UNTITLED

BREAKING HER RULES

RULES OF LOVE

DEIDRE - ANN ANDERSON

OTHER BOOKS BY DEIDRE – ANN ANDERSON:

CONSUMED BY HEAT TRILOGY

Sparked

Ignited

Engulfed

Falling For Heat - (Clean Version of The Trilogy as A Standalone)

NIGHT CAP NOVELLAS:

Willed to a Dom

The Dom She Needed

RULES OF LOVE SERIES

Changing Her Rules

Breaking Her Rules

Bending Her Rules

CHAPTER 1

KAMILLA

*I*n order to survive in a friends-with-benefits situation, you need to abide by three simple rules:

1. Never select someone you work with or who could fire you.
2. Never select someone that lives in your neighborhood.

And my personal favorite:

1. NEVER EVER FALL IN LOVE!

THESE RULES ARE ETCHED in the back of my mind as a loud, throaty moan jolts me from my sleep. I groan, pulling a pillow over my head in a futile attempt to muffle the sounds coming from the room next to mine.

Not again.

The rhythmic creaking of bedsprings and breathy cries of pleasure pound against my skull like a jackhammer. I glance at the alarm clock on my nightstand and groan once more. Based on the angry red numbers it is only 3 AM.

Are you fucking serious, Jackson? There is no bloody way I'm dealing with this a third time in one week.

Anger coils in my stomach as I lay there listening to the show my roommate is starring in. We have rules, damn it. No bringing random women over when I'm home, and definitely no loud sex marathons in the middle of the night.

I sigh, flopping onto my back and staring up at the ceiling. The moans and groans coming through the wall make it impossible to sleep, and I know from experience that yelling at him to keep it down will only encourage his exhibitionist tendencies.

Why the fuck did I think living with Jackson was a good idea again?

Oh right, I didn't. But I had been broke and stupid enough to believe his charm and good looks made up for his complete lack of respect for other people's boundaries.

Lesson learned.

I glance over at the clock again, cursing under my breath. At this rate, I'll be exhausted for my 8 AM client, and the last thing I need is to be off my game to deal with Chelsea. Chelsea's hard enough to deal with on a good day, never mind when I'm running on only three hours of sleep.

Unless Chelsea's the one Jackson is so loudly destroying in the next room, then all bets are off.

The bedsprings stop creaking, and a feminine cry of pleasure fills the silence. I grab my pillow again and press it over my head, trying to block out the sounds as the girl's orgasm shakes the walls of my bedroom.

This is the last straw. Jackson's gonna have to get an earful in the morning, and if he doesn't shape up then I'm done. I can't be the unwilling audience to his endless sexcapades anymore.

Something has to change before I lose my mind. Even if I have to get a lousy match box studio apartment close to my clinic.

I toss and turn for a while longer before giving up on sleep altogether. Might as well get an early start to the day. Sighing, I push my log of a body off the bed and pull on an oversized T-shirt to cover my ass before making my way to caffeine.

When I emerge from my room, my nose crinkles in distaste as I take in the mess that is our living room. Empty beer bottles litter the coffee table, and remnants of snacks are ground into the carpet.

And draped over my prized Espresso machine like a fucking obscene flag is a pair of lacy red panties.

My eye twitches.

That! Is! It!

I storm over to the espresso machine and yank the panties off. My lips press into a thin angry line. How dare he violate the one sacred space I have in this apartment? My Espresso machine is off-limits.

Clenching the panties in my fist, I stride over to Jackson's bedroom and pound on the door.

"Jackson! Get your ass out here right now," I yell.

No response. The nerve.

I pound against the door again. This time harder than before.

"Jackson, I mean it! We need to talk, and you better be decent when you come out here."

Again, no response.

Fuming, I march back to my bedroom, rip a page from the notepad on my bedside table, and begin crafting a letter giving Jackson, and his disgusting guest, a piece of my mind.

*J*ACKSON,

Since you refuse to answer the door even though I know you can fucking hear me. Let me remind you for the eighteenth fucking time. YOU DO NOT LIVE HERE ALONE!   The last thing I need to see after being kept up all night from your theatrical moans is dirty frigging underwear in the kitchen OR ON MY ESPRESSO MACHINE. Especially after I cleaned up the kitchen before I went to bed.

How about you gag your 'pick of the day' next time to shut them up? And while you're at it, have them keep their dirty drawers off my belongings.

Your annoyed roommate,
Kamilla

STILL FUMING, I march back over to Jackson's bedroom then stuff both the panties and letter through a crack that has now magically appeared in his door.

I turn away from Jackson's door, content with my small victory. Releasing a calming breath, I head back to my bedroom, refusing to allow Jackson's asshole tendencies to ruin my entire day. I have a long day ahead and clients who depend on me to be focused and composed.

Sighing, I grab my towel. A long hot shower will do me good. I ignore the pang of annoyance that hits me as I walk past Jackson's now-closed door again on my way to our shared bathroom.

Once in the shower, I allow the warm water to cascade over my body, washing away the tension and frustration from the whole situation with Jackson and all that pisses me off about him. His arrogant smirk and constant condescending words echo in my mind as I lather lavender scented body wash over my skin.

Breathe in. Breathe out.

I push the toxic thoughts out of my mind and refocus on all I need to do to get ready for work. As a physiotherapist, my patients depend on me to be attentive. So, Jackson's daily antics are the last thing I need to stick with me throughout the day.

Grabbing my towel, I step out of the shower and pat myself dry while studying my sleep-deprived reflection. In the foggy mirror, my reflection stares back at me - dark brown skin, ample breasts, and a determined set to my jaw.

I draw in a deep breath and repeat my daily affirmations.

"I'm strong. I'm powerful. I won't allow anyone to make me feel small. Especially not the asshole I happen to live with."

With that resolve strengthening my spine, I start my morning makeup routine. Primer, foundation, and concealer to hide the signs of stress and lack of sleep. Eye shadow, eyeliner, and mascara make my eyes pop. Golden blush and brown lipstick for a natural glow.

With my makeup almost done, I wrap myself tighter with the towel and return to my bedroom as it bakes. The end half of a chat notification goes off as I enter my room, alerting me that the Sisterhood chat is awake.

The Sisterhood is my second family. My three best girls, Trina, Latalia, and Natasha. They're never afraid to tell me what I need to hear, even if I won't like it.

TRINA:

Rise and grind bitches! Time to get this money.

LATALIA:

Yawns. Too early Trina. Some of us value our beauty sleep.

NATASHA:

I'm with Tals on this one. Can we start the chat later? My brain isn't functioning yet.

Me:

Good morning, ladies! I'm up and getting ready. In fact, I'm almost ready for work. We have bills to pay and success to achieve.

TRINA:

Atta girl Kam! That's the motivation we need.

Me:

Besides some of us have assholes they're trying to get away from. Plus, there is zero sleep in my future here with Sir Fucks-a-lot back to his usual antics.

TRINA:

Oh no! What did that wannabe Loverboy do this time? I say we all go over there and give him a piece of our minds with very few words.

LATALIA:

Tri! No violence. Use your words.

Me:

I love you hoes. But I'm fine. Honestly. Jackson's idiocy isn't worth my time or energy. I have too many important things to focus on.

NATASHA:

Look at you go with that positive attitude so early in the AM! You're too good to be stressing over that asshole anyway. And to think we initially thought his sexy ass body would translate to his personality. Forget about him and go slay your day.

TRINA:

Oh, make no mistake, he may be a gigantic asshole but that asshole sure is fine.

LATALIA:

Lol. I would not know. I only got eyes for the man in my bed.

NATASHA:

Bitch, please. Blaine is right beside you, isn't he? Tell him morning for us.

LATALIA:

He is. But that is beside the point.

THAT MAKES ME LAUGH, Latalia and Blaine tied the knot a few months ago, and we all know she's 'goo goo ga ga' over her man. But even I could admit Jackson is more than easy on the eyes, and I hated his guts.

Me:
Y'all are crazy, you know that.

TRINA:

Of course, our asses are all crazy, but that's why you love us. We keep the spice in your life.

Me:

lol. Sure do. Thanks, guys. Nat got it right. The plan is to ignore my roommate and get to that cash. Now get all your asses up and get to work! All of you! The path to success won't walk itself!

LATALIA:

Yes mother!

Me:

lol. I'll check in later. Bye bitches.

THE SUPPORT and humor from my friends always bolster my mood and motivation I need to make the coin needed to get out of here and into my own place. Jackson may try to get under my skin, but he will never break me. I head to the kitchen with a smile on my face. Nothing is gonna ruin my day. I won't let it.

The ingredients to my usual 'on the go' smoothie are ready and waiting in the container I left them in after meal prepping last night. I grab them and turn to the blender to find a piece of folded paper between the blender and the Espresso machine. I ignore it. It wasn't there earlier so it's no doubt an antagonistic response from my dear frustrating roommate.

Determined, I proceed to add my chopped kale and berries to

the blender with a cup of milk and move to turn it on but pause, glancing at the letter once more.

Maybe I should just check the letter.

What if his 'pick of the week' fucked with my blender too, and this is his weird way of telling me because he knows my morning routine.

I sigh, knowing in the back of my mind I should just ignore Jackson's foolishness, but curiosity gets the better of me. I unfold the letter and instantly wish I hadn't.

My jaw falls open as I read.

My Dearest Kamilla,

Thank you for taking time out of your busy day to inform my guest how "melodious" she sounded last night. I was sure to let her know that coming from you that was a compliment as hopefully that meant she may have inspired you to clear out the cobwebs that currently reside between your legs.

What I do in my apartment is none of your business. So, I would suggest you get yourself a pair of headphones. That is unless you are much more of a freak than you are willing to admit to yourself.

Your Loving Roomie,

Jackson

What in the actual fuck?

Cobwebs?

My hands clench into fists, crumpling the vile letter. How dare he speak to me this way? I should march right over there and -

No. I draw in a deep breath and release my anger as I breathe out. This is what he wants. Jackson wants a reaction from me. He feeds off drama and contention like a leech sucking blood, I refuse to give him the satisfaction.

Instead of marching over to Jackson's room like I really want to, I go back to blending my smoothie, trying and failing to ignore Jackson's words that are still carving their way through my mind.

I take a few more calming breaths in an attempt to well the anger with very little success. All the breaths do is make the rage in my gut flare hotter. That arrogant, infuriating man gets on my fucking nerves. How dare he speak to me like that?

I pour my smoothie out into my travel tumbler, anger coursing through my veins.

"You know what, fuck the high road," I whisper to myself.

With trembling fingers, I grab a pen and flip his stupid note over to scrawl my response before I can talk myself out of it.

DEAR JACKSON,

Why don't you go do what you do best and go fuck yourself?
Your Concerned Roommate,
Kamilla.

I SHOVE the note under Jackson's door and storm out of the apartment, slamming the door behind me. The summer air is humid and oppressive, matching my mood to a tee.

My phone buzzes in my pocket before I've even made it to the parking lot. I yank it out, knowing who the text will be from.

JACKSON:

Your letter was hilarious. Let's not kid ourselves here, Kammie. The only person you would like me to go fuck is you.

. . .

"Arrogant bastard," I mutter under my breath. "Like I would ever."

I shake my head and tap out a response, refusing to give him the satisfaction of riling me up further.

> *Me:*
> *Remind me to find you a good psychiatrist, because clearly, you're delusional.*

With that, I silence my phone and climb into my car, cranking up the AC and radio to drown out my anger and frustration. Jackson might be my roommate, but he's also the most infuriating man I've ever known. The sooner I can move out of that apartment, the better.

CHAPTER 2

JACKSON

There are three rules to abide by when trying not to cross the line with your best friend's sister:

1. Keep her believing you're always fucking someone else. Most times, this alone will keep women at bay. Or at least the type of woman I actually want around for more than just a good time.
2. Avoid physical contact of all kinds, but especially anything that can be perceived as sexual. You can't fuck without touching, right?

And my personal favorite:

1. Keep her pissed off at you. Okay, fine, this one isn't exactly necessary, but again in most cases if a woman is pissed off at you there's no way in hell she's letting you

close enough to her to fuck her. Unless you both like hate sex. Then all bets are off

The door slams behind Kamilla, rattling the walls in the penthouse. On queue, I lower the volume on the porno I had on a loop throughout the night and power off the flat screen, the moans and grunts cutting off mid-thrust.

This is becoming a nightly act. I scrub a hand over my face, guilt gnawing at my insides. If Kamilla only knew I wasn't really fucking anyone, she'd flip. I haven't been with a woman since Kamilla moved in almost a year ago when Luis all but begged me to give her a place to stay. Right before threatening my life if I even thought of fucking his sister.

I had agreed, of course, but that was before I saw how much of a woman she'd become. Kamilla is not only gorgeous, she's spunky, intelligent, driven, and can cook circles around my own mother. In theory, she ticks all my boxes. Problem is one of those boxes vetoes the rest.

My promise to Luis is bullshit. There's no way I can keep my hands off Kamilla long-term if she keeps living here. But there's also no way in hell, I'm putting her out on the street without somewhere stable to go.

Luis is my best friend though, and I won't betray his trust. I can't. Cursing, I glance up at the clock and push from the bed. The scent of Kamilla's perfume lingers in the air, tormenting me. I slam my fist into the wall, pain shooting up my arm. Fuck, not even the pain can help get her out of my head.

Sighing, I head to the shower and turn it on cold. This is torture. I step in, the freezing water pounding over my tense muscles. I lean back into it, Kamilla's essence fading under the assault of the chill and moisture. My cock aches, still hard as steel from the ever-playing fantasy of Kamilla in my mind. I wrap my hand around it, stroking in slow motion.

I picture Kamilla in my mind, her full lips parted, chest heaving. I groan, my strokes picking up speed. Our near kiss plays on a loop, I imagine the feel of her in my arms, the softness of her body molding with mine.

I'm close, so close. My hand moves faster as I imagine sliding inside her tight, wet heat.

"Kamilla," I groan, coming hard, her name a prayer on my lips.

Guilt washes over me in the aftermath. I can't keep doing this. I made a promise to Luis that I intend to keep, no matter how much it kills me. Kamilla is off-limits.

Always.

I turn off the water and step out of the shower on shaky legs. Looks like I need to add a new rule to my list.

Rule #4 - Don't think about your best friend's sister when you jerk off.

"Yep, that should do it," I mutter, sarcasm lacing every word.

Who am I kidding? I'm so fucked.

Wrapping a towel around my waist, I avoid my reflection in the mirror. If I see the hunger in my eyes, the need written all over my face, I'll drive right up to Kamilla's clinic and take what I want.

What we both want.

I yank on a pair of football shorts and a tank top, running a hand through my damp hair. My shoulder throbs where I took a hit in practice yesterday, the ugly bruise a battle wound of purple and green that I wear proudly. As long as I can still move without gripping pain, I'm still good to go.

The doorbell rings, and I freeze, pulse kicking. Kamilla shouldn't be back for hours, and she has a key. And I'm not in a mental state for surprise company. I stride to the entryway and fling open the door, ready to tell whoever's on the other side to fuck off.

But when I get there, I don't. It's the delivery guy with a Victoria Secret bag.

Shit, I'd completely forgotten. I get these Victoria Secret deliveries every few days set at a time I know Kamilla will have already left for work. Yet another tiny detail of sticking to rule number three.

I take the bag with a muttered thanks and shut the door, peeking inside. Another lacey Teddy, crotchless panties. But this one is in black.

A growl rumbles in my throat as I stick them on Kamilla's room door handle. Now I just have to get back in time to see the fury on her face when she finds them, the fire in her eyes as she realizes I left them there to torment her.

My fingers curl into the lacy fabric. An image of Kamilla wearing them fills my mind and I slam my eyes shut, drawing in a breath.

Think of someone else. Anything else.

Football. Housework. What I'll have for dinner.

Luis. Think of Luis.

Anything but Kamilla in those panties, waiting for me in her bed. I stuff the now empty bag in my duffle and scrub both hands over my face.

Fuck. It's been months of this torture. How the fuck am I going to last the rest of the year we agreed to be roommates. Sighing I throw the strap of my duffle over my shoulder. I need to get out of here before I do something stupid.

I race out the front door and jump into my truck in the parking lot, turning the radio up loud. Anything to drown out the thoughts in my head.

By the time I get to the field, I've almost convinced myself I can keep my promise to stay away from Kamilla. To not touch her. Then I see Luis coming toward me as I get out of my truck, and my stomach twists into knots.

"Hey man," he calls.

I force a smile. "Hey Luis, what's up?"

"Just another day, you know," he responds, slapping me on my bruised shoulder. "Hey, you never did tell me how things worked out with Kam yesterday. She seemed pretty pissed when I spoke to her this morning. Everything good over there with y'all?"

A flash of the red lace I'd planted on her prized Espresso machine blazes through my mind, and I clench my jaw. "Everything's peachy," I grit out.

"Really?" Luis studies me, brows drawing together. "Cause you seem tense bro. And I know my sister can be a handful when she decides to push buttons no one needs her pushing."

That makes me smile. If he only knew I'm the only one in that apartment doing the button pushing. That's the one part of having Kamilla in my apartment that I'm actually enjoying.

"I'm good." I turn away, grabbing my helmet and pads from the truck bed. "Let's just get to practice."

Luis is silent for a beat, then sighs. "I really appreciate all you're doing to help my sister out man, having Kam in your space and all. So, I'm happy you two are making it work."

As we walk onto the field, he bumps my shoulder with his. "But if you need to talk about any of my sister's antics, you know where to find me."

Guilt twists in my gut. I wish I could tell him the truth, but I can't. I'm struggling every damn day not to throw his little sister down on the kitchen counter, couch, or her bed and fuck her senseless.

I swallow hard and nod. "Yeah. Thanks, man."

We fall into our usual drills, and I draw on the familiarity to push the inappropriate thoughts of Kamilla out of my mind. At least I try.

Sweat trickles down my neck as I sprint across the field, dodging offensive linemen trying to block me. My heart pounds with a mix of determination to complete the play and adrenaline as nothing will stop me from getting to my mark. A flash of black hair, and smooth, brown skin enters my mind, my stride faltering for a split second.

Fuck. Kamilla?

The image of her in a football jersey and nothing else makes my mouth go dry.

I crash into a wall of muscle and collapse onto the green, bringing three of my teammates down with me as they try and fail to jump over my limbs. Pain explodes in my groin as one of their bodies lands on top of my hip. And I cry out as another land on my shoulder.

"Shit. You okay man?" The guy that fell on my shoulder asks as he stands, hovering over me. Concern etches on the other's face as he eases off my groin, gripping his shoulder.

I grimace, clutching my shoulder with my good arm as I try to sit up.

"Yeah, I'm good," I lie. *Good at messing up the one thing I'm passionate about. Sure.*

I shake my head, cursing under my breath. I can't get Kamilla out of my mind, no matter how hard I try. My promise to Luis wars with my attraction to his sister, her pull as strong as gravity even in the times when it's the last thing I need distracting me. If I don't get this out of my system somehow, soon, it's going to be the death of me.

Coach blows the whistle, yelling at us to take a break. I stay on the ground, staring up at the clouds while my team heads to the benches. How the fuck am I supposed to resist Kamilla when even the very thought of her shatters my focus?

I'm playing with fire here, and if I'm not careful, I'll be the one burned. Badly. But the fantasy of her lips on mine, the need to feel her body pressed against me, ignites an ache inside that won't quit. I'm in deep shit. The kind that could cost me everything, my friendship with Luis and the gel of my whole team.

All for one woman.

One woman I can't stop thinking about.

Fuck, I need to stand. I push back up to a sitting position and push upwards to my knees, a loud curse escaping my lips as pain shoots upwards from my groin to connect with my shoulder.

My teammates crowd around me, their worried voices blending together.

"Should we call the medic?" One asks.

"Do you need help getting up?" asks another.

I grit my teeth against the pain. "I'm fine. Just give me a minute."

Luis kneels beside me, brows drawn together as he studies me. "You sure, man? That looked bad."

"Really, I'm okay," I lie again.

The last thing I need is Luis fussing over me like a mother hen. I brace for the pain and push up on shaky legs. I sway a bit before finding my balance.

"You don't look okay," Luis says. "I think you ought to let me take you to get checked out."

"I said I'm fine," I bite back, shrugging out of his grasp. I regret it as soon as I do. Sharp pain lance through my shoulder again.

Luis's eyes narrow. "Since when are you too stubborn to admit you're hurt?"

He reaches for my arm, and I jerk away.

"Damn it, Luis, just drop it," I yell at him.

Silence falls over the field as my teammates stare between us. Luis rears back, hurt flashing across his face before his expression hardens.

"Fuck it," he says, his tone rigid. "Do what you want."

With that, he turns on his heels and stalks off, leaving a bitter taste in my mouth. I've never snapped at Luis like that before. guilt twists my gut as I watch him go, I'm not upset with him. But there's no way in fuck I can explain what just happened to a medic with Luis next to me. He'd only cling onto the reason I was so distracted in the first place. Right now, our friendship is just as injured as my body because of one stupid and careless moment. I sigh, Luis's ego is just another thing I can stick on my list of shit I've managed to screw up this morning.

I trudge into the locker room, gritting my teeth against the pain. I need to get out of here. As much as I can't afford to have Luis be the one to take me to see a doc, I know I need a check-up. The problem is there's no way I'll be able to drive like this.

With a sigh, I pull out my phone to call the one person I know who will come with no questions asked. As much as she may hate me, she's the type of person that can't bear to see people hurt. The same person who caused the injury in the first place. Kamilla. I can admit she's the last person I should be calling right now, but there are very few options for discretion from my teammates.

The phone rings twice before she answers, her voice warm and laced with sass.

"What the hell do you want now Jackson? Didn't you get enough said about my cobwebs earlier? Or are you calling to take me up on an offer for the psychiatrist?"

I swallow hard to stop myself from responding with a smart retort. I hate that I have to be crawling to her for a favor right now.

"I need your help," I manage to spit out.

The line goes silent.

"Look, I kind of got injured at practice today. I was hoping you could give me a ride to the emergency room at your clinic."

Again silence.

"Wait, how badly are you hurt," she asks. "wouldn't it be quicker to get someone there to drop you here? Do you need me to call Luis? I'm sure he'll -"

"No," I say, cutting her off. "I can't get into it, but I need you."

Silence. Then, "Of course. I'll be right there." Her tone is all business, the usual sassy lilt gone. I end the call and sink onto the locker room bench, head in my hands.

How did I get into this mess?

I had one task. To keep Kamilla at a distance for both our sakes and for Luis's. That's why I have those stupid rules. Yet here I am, about to be at her mercy. Alone in a car with her for the painstakingly long ride to the clinic. When it comes to Kamilla Morallez, my self-control is a joke.

I made a promise to Luis, and I still intend to keep it. But one look into those dark brown eyes and every noble intention in my body travels out the window. Resisting her is harder than I'd ever imagined but I am Jackson Fucking Taylor, and there's no way in hell I'm going to allow one woman to break me.

Especially not the only one that's off-limits.

CHAPTER 3

KAMILLA

I park my car outside the practice field where Luis and Jackson spend most of their time, reluctant to step out into the blazing heat of the sun. As expected, Jackson is nowhere to be seen. Unwilling to get scorched for a prick, I pull my phone out and dial Jackson's number.

No answer.

I call again, cursing when yet again it rings out to voicemail.

Sighing, I decide to make my way inside the practice grounds. The last thing I want is to prolong this ordeal. I'd wanted so badly to tell Jackson to go call his 'pick of the week' to get him, but he'd sounded so damn solemn, and I wouldn't be able to live with myself knowing someone called me in a medical crisis and I told them to piss off.

"Jackson," I call out, shielding my eyes from the harsh sunlight as I enter the field gates.

No response.

Gritting my teeth, I continue walking, scanning the area for any sign of Jackson.

"Kamilla?" A familiar voice calls out.

My heart sinks as I turn to face my older brother, Luis. Luis had given me an earful about 'protocol' when I first moved in with Jackson. Never mind the fact that this whole living arrangement was his stupid doing in the first place.

"What are you doing here?" Luis asks, closing the space between us.

"Hey Luis," I say, trying to sound casual. "I seem to be your friend's choice of chauffeur. He said he got injured on the field and needs a ride to the clinic."

"Luis raises an eyebrow. "Did he, now? Why didn't he just ask me for a ride?"

I shrug, feeling a tad defensive in response to his tone. "I don't know, Luis. Why don't you ask him? He called me, so here I am. Not that I can say the same for him, and I honestly don't have time for all this right now."

"Alright," Luis says, his tone softening. "Just seems a bit strange, that's all. You two aren't exactly close. "

"True," I admit, not wanting to get into it with Luis. "But to be fair, you're the one who insisted on us living together and helping each other out in the first place, remember? So can we please just drop it?"

"Fine, fine," Luis relents, holding up his hands in surrender. "I just worry about you, you know that."

"I know," I say, smiling at him. "And I appreciate it. But as I keep telling you, I can handle myself."

"Of course, you can," Luis agrees, giving me a quick hug. "You're strong. You always have been. Just...be careful, alright? Jackson may be my best friend, but he can be a dog sometimes. Especially when it comes to sleeping around."

"Now that's real rich coming from you," I say, laughing. "Y'all are literally two peas in a pod."

Luis fakes hurt as he grips his chest and stumbles backward.

"Please, you know it's true. Now, can you please help me find Jackson so I can get this over with."

"Alright," Luis says, a grin spreading across his face as we set off together in search of Jackson.

The lightness in the air doesn't last long as I still sense Luis's unease as we walk through the practice grounds. I fight the urge to roll my eyes, the tension in the air is all in Luis's head. Jackson is not running short in the women's department. Even my sleep-deprived eyes know that.

"I'm sorry but I gotta ask the obvious," Luis finally says, his voice low and serious, "is there something going on between you and Jackson that I don't know about?"

I stop in my tracks, taken aback by his question. "Something like...?"

"Come on, Kamilla," he replies, looking at me with an intensity I've rarely seen from him. "You're picking him up from practice, helping him out when he's injured... It seems like more than just a friendly gesture."

"Are you serious right now?" I scoff, trying and failing to hide my annoyance. "Three seconds ago, you were asking why he didn't just ask you to take him. Is there something going on between you two I should know about?" Luis glares at me, but I stand my ground. "Just because I'm helping him doesn't mean there's something going on between us. And, even if there was, it's none of your business."

"Alright, alright," Luis says, raising his hands in surrender. "I'm just looking out for you, sis."

"Ugh, I'm sick of people telling me what to do and who to associate with," I mutter under my breath, my frustration growing. My thoughts are interrupted when I see Jackson limping toward us from behind Luis.

'Hey, guys," Jackson calls out, a slight grimace on his face as he approaches us. "Thanks for coming, Kamilla."

"Uh-huh," I reply, still irked by Luis's insinuations. I cross my arms and narrow my eyes at Jackson. "What the hell happened to you and why couldn't you have found anyone else to take you to the clinic?"

Jackson glances between Luis and me, clearly sensing the tension. "Sorry, I didn't mean to cause any trouble. I just thought it'd be easier since you work there and all. Figured I'd get a leg in without waiting for hours to see someone."

"Whatever," I huff, not wanting to prolong the conversation. "Let's just get going, then."

Luis pulls Jackson aside before he can leave, making my blood boil. "What really was this man?"

"Oh, fuck this" I snap, my patience wearing thin. "As I said to you before even if there was something going on between Jackson and me, which for the millionth time there isn't, it would be none of your fucking business." I glare at him. "And don't forget you were the one who pinned me on him in the first place. If you didn't want us interacting you should've helped me when I needed it. instead of pawning me off."

Luis raises his hands defensively, but I can see the concern still etched on his face. Jackson steps in then, trying to smooth things over. "Kamilla's right, man. There's nothing going on between us. We're just friends if you can even call it that, and she's helping me out as a favor. You don't need to worry about anything."

A twinge of disappointment gnaws at me from Jackson's words, even though I know they're true. Shaking off the feeling, I focus on the task at hand. "Come on, Jackson, let's go. The sooner we get to the clinic, the sooner you can get checked out and we can put this whole thing behind us."

As we walk towards my car, I can feel Luis's eyes on us. I shoot him one last annoyed glance before climbing into the driver's seat and starting the engine. As I pull away from the curb, the strange tension that has developed between Jackson and me since this whole ordeal began isn't lost on me. But the last thing I need is to acknowledge it and prove Luis right.

"Sorry about all that," Jackson whispers from the passenger seat, rubbing the back of his neck. "Luis can be pretty overprotective sometimes, huh?"

"Yeah, I'm sure the whole world has noticed that by now," I reply, my tone dry.

I keep my eyes set on the road. My mind, however, is racing with thoughts of what might have been if things had been different, and whether or not Luis is right and there could be something more between Jackson and me.

"Right," Jackson agrees, flashing me a warm grin that makes my stomach flip despite the frustration swirling inside of me.

The tension inside the car is palpable, a heavy weight pressing down on both of us. I can't help but steal a few glances at Jackson, his strong jawline set and dark blue eyes fixed forward. I find myself wondering what he's thinking about and if it's anything like the whirlwind of emotions that are stirring within me.

"Seriously, Kamilla," Jackson says, breaking the silence. "I don't know why Luis made such a big fuss. It's not like you and I have anything going on."

"True," I respond, trying to sound nonchalant. "But even if we did, he has no right to pry like that. I'm a grown-ass woman. What I decide to do and who I sleep with is no one's concern but my own."

"Exactly," Jackson agrees, nodding. He hesitates for a moment before adding, "Besides, it's not like you're really my type, anyway."

My heart drops at his words, a wave of anger washing over me. Though whatever led him to that conclusion is merely an assumption as he barely knows me. I grip the steering wheel tighter, grateful for my dark skin stopping him from seeing my knuckles turning white.

"And what type would I be?" I ask, my voice sharp and cold.

"And you better think before you answer because if you answer with anything outside of educated and beautiful, you're gonna have more injuries to nurse."

I laugh, but it's bitter.

Jackson seems taken aback by my reaction, his eyes widening in surprise. "I just meant... well, you know, you're not the kind of girl I usually go for."

"Really?" I snap, my anger boiling over. "And what kind of girl would that be? Someone who fawns over you and hangs on to your every word? Someone who doesn't challenge you or push you to be a better person? Because I was under the impression that your type was anything with a pulse from how frequently you make booty calls."

Jackson sighs. "Calm down, I didn't mean it like that." I glance over to find Jackson's face flushed. "I guess I just meant that, well, you're different from the girls I've dated in the past."

"Damn right, I'm different," I retort, my voice shaking a tad. "I'm a whole lotta woman, and I wouldn't expect someone like you to know how to appreciate that."

"What's that does that mean?" Jackson asks, turning to see my face and flinching.

"Exactly what it sounds like. I don't need your approval or validation to know my worth, Jackson. And if you think for one second that I'm going to let you walk all over me just because I happen to be living in your apartment, then you've got another thing coming."

"I never said you weren't," he admits. "You know exactly who you are. That's actually one of the few things I don't hate about you." He sighs. "I wasn't trying to insult you, I'm sorry if I did. I was just saying Luis has nothing to worry about. That's all."

I take a deep breath, trying to quell the anger that still simmers beneath the surface. Jackson must really be in pain to be apologizing. I remind myself now is not the time to be arguing about something so trivial.

"Fine," I say finally, my voice low and steady. "Apology accepted. But let's just focus on getting you to the clinic, alright?"

"Alright," Jackson agrees, nodding. "And for what it's worth, Kamilla, I really do appreciate everything you're doing for me."

"Consider it payback for me not getting any more scandalous surprises on my Espresso machine," I reply, offering him a small smile.

Jackson chokes out a laugh. "No violence to the coffee machine. You have my word."

As we continue our drive to the clinic, the tension between us begins to dissipate, but in its place lies an unspoken understanding: there are some lines that shouldn't be crossed, and some comments that are better left unsaid.

"Do you need me to go in with you to the doctor on call," I ask as I pull into the clinic.

Jackson doesn't respond. I glance over to see him on his phone. I park and shut off the engine.

"Hey," I say, lightly tapping him on his leg, and ignoring the sudden surge that flows through me at the contact. Jackson looks up at me and I pull my hand away.

"Am I taking you into the doctor's office?" I say again.

His expression falls. "Oh no, no. I don't want to put you out any further. I got it from here."

I nod, a pang of unwarranted sadness filling me as he slides out of the car, flinching.

'Are you sure you don't need me to -" My question falls short as the real reason he no longer needs my help comes into view. All 5 ft 4- ish inches of her.

I fight the urge to roll my eyes and scoff.

"Close my door, Jackson," I say with more bitterness in my tone than intended.

He does, and I drive off to my assigned parking spot. Not bothering to ask him any further questions.

CHAPTER 4

JACKSON

The sterile smell of the clinic fills my nostrils as I sit on the cold examination table, waiting for the doctor to return with my X-ray results. Its chilly touch seeps through the thin barrier of the paper gown, grounding me to the harsh reality of my situation. The bright fluorescent lights overhead cast a harsh glow on my bruised and battered body.

Dr. Peterson, a figure of stoic professionalism, strides back into the room, his crisp white lab coat billowing in the breeze of the fan. "Alright, Jackson," he says, his voice a resonant, unwavering note in the tense quiet of the room. He gestures to the X-rays in his grasp, a web of bone and shadow cast onto the illuminated screen. "Your x-rays show a hairline fracture in your right shoulder and serious bruising in your groin," Dr. Peterson says, pulling me back into the moment. "You also have some muscle strains and bruising around the area. It's going to take some time to heal, but I think we can speed up the process with a targeted treatment plan."

A jolt of pain flares through my shoulder as I shift on the table, the seemingly innocuous movement now laden with discomfort. I manage to bite back a groan, my eyes fixed on the doctor. "What kind of treatments are we looking at, Doc?"

"Rest will be essential," he replies, his tone matter of fact. "As well as physiotherapy. Physio will help you regain strength and mobility in the injured area. And I know just the person for the job."

"Who?" I ask, trying to ignore the sinking feeling in my gut that tells me I already know the answer.

"Kamilla Morallez," Dr. Peterson responds, confirming my suspicions. "She's one of the best physiotherapists in our network, specializing in sports-related injuries. She's worked with several professional athletes before, so she's more than qualified to help you get back on track."

"Kamilla?" My voice strains around her name, each syllable heavy with the kaleidoscope of emotions – lust and frustration – that seem to surge through my veins. It's a cruel irony as she's the reason for my battered state in the first place.

"Trust me, Jackson," Dr. Peterson reassures me. "Ms. Morallez's skills and experience make her the perfect fit for your situation. I've seen her work wonders with clients who had similar injuries."

With a deep sigh, I thread my fingers through my tousled hair, my mind racing. "Doctor, I appreciate your recommendation, but working with Kamilla might not be as straightforward as you think," I admit, my rules and promise hanging over me like a dark cloud. "See I know her, and our affiliation might make things... complicated."

Dr. Peterson raises an eyebrow, his expression thoughtful. "Jackson, I understand that you two may have had some personal differences in the past, but this is about your recovery. You need the best treatment possible, and Kamilla is the best physiotherapist for your specific injuries."

As he speaks, I recall her confident stride and the way she commanded respect from everyone around her. It's true that Kamilla is exceptional at what she does, but our current entanglements could easily jeopardize any professional relationship we could have.

"Doctor, it's not about her qualifications or expertise," I attempt to explain, grappling for the right words to convey my apprehension. "We've had some... let's say, disagreements. I'm concerned it could hinder our working relationship."

Dr. Peterson nods slowly, his eyes never leaving mine. "I see. Well, Jackson, I can only remind you that Kamilla has dealt with similar cases to yours, including working with athletes with demanding schedules. She'll also be familiar with your initial medical visit being in the same clinic, which means she can tailor your treatment plan more effectively than someone new to your case."

His words strike a chord within me, and I find myself nodding in agreement. He's right – Kamilla's familiarity with my medical background would be invaluable during my recovery process. But still, the thought of working so closely with her sends a shiver down my spine.

"Alright, Doc," I concede, swallowing my reservations. "I'll give it a shot. But I want to speak to her first. I need to make sure we can maintain a professional relationship despite our current affiliation."

"Of course," Dr. Peterson agrees, giving me a reassuring smile. "The decision of who you work with is solely yours to make, I can only give you my recommendation. But remember Jackson, this is about what's best for your recovery so give Kamilla a fair chance, alright?"

"Alright," I reply, my voice barely above a whisper.

Dr. Peterson nods before turning to hand me a black sling. "Until you start with Ms. Morallez, I need you to avoid strenuous activity and rest your shoulder. The sling should help to avoid painful stray movements of the joint."

"Thanks, doc," I say as the doctor leaves the room. I take a deep breath, steeling myself for the conversation I'm about to have. I slide off the table and get dressed before grabbing my phone and dialing Luis's number.

"Yo," Luis answers on the first ring. "So, did the doc say you only have a few days to live."

I laugh. "He may as well have."

I press the phone against my ear and tie the strings on my shorts. "I need your help with something."

"Sure, man. What's up?" Luis replies, his voice sounding concerned.

"The doctor recommended that I work with a physiotherapist to recover." I pause, my heart pounding in my chest. "And just my luck, he suggested Kamilla."

"Kamilla?" Luis echoes, surprised.

"Exactly, my thought when he said it" I admit, running a hand through my hair. "But she's apparently an excellent physiotherapist, and the doctor thinks she'd be perfect for my case. But I think I may have just used up my one favor by asking her to drop me here. Plus, she wasn't too pleased when she saw Chelsea waiting for me when we got to the clinic. But I need a ride home and Chelsea offered."

"So, you want me to mediate? Okay, let me handle this," Luis replies, his voice echoing the steady calm I've come to rely on. "I'll talk to her, see where she stands on the matter. But first, level with me bro. Tell me you didn't go back on your word and screwed around with my sister.

"I swear to you there's nothing to worry about on that front." I sigh. "To be honest with you man, Kamilla hates my guts. I admit I haven't exactly made it easier for her to live with me. I know that. All I can do, at this point, is explain how important my recovery is to me and that her expertise would really make a difference. Hopefully, that along with you chatting with her will get her on board."

"Sounds like a solid plan," Luis adds. "Just don't fuck me over man. If there's any chance of you two getting together, I'd prefer you just rip the Band-Aid."

"Of course," I reply, my voice steady. "I'll lay everything on the same table I lay her on."

I laughed but Luis didn't.

"Too soon?" I tease.

"It'll always be too soon for that," Luis warns, his voice an uncomfortable blend of irritation and unease. "I'll have a talk with her and let you know where we stand. Just be prepared for any outcome."

"Alright man. Thanks. I appreciate it," I say. "Anyway, I got Chelsea waiting. So, I better get going."

Luis agrees and I hang up the phone.

As I step out of the confines of the clinic and draw in a deep breath. The world outside the clinic is a riot of colors - pink and white blossoms on the trees nearby, their sweet scent acting as a balm to my frayed nerves, washing away the stray scent of antiseptic that clings to me.

Squinting against the brilliant glow, I spot Chelsea. I'm still not sure this is my greatest idea. Chelsea and I are stuck in this weird on-again-off-again 'fuck and go' relationship. One that I could agree ended months ago as we generally hooked up in my apartment and it just didn't feel right after Kamilla moved in. But in Chelsea's head, that arrangement is still alive and kicking regardless of how many times I shut it down.

Sighing, I push forward. Chelsea is leaning against the polished metallic body of her expensive sports car, cherry-red and gleaming under the sun's rays. Her red lipstick matches it perfectly. A predatory smile tugs at her lips, her teeth gleaming in an unnatural white.

Hey, handsome," Chelsea drawls, pushing off from the car as I approach. The soft click-clack of her high heels on the paved lot harmonizes with the distant buzz of the city. Each calculated, swinging step she takes is meant to mesmerize, as her golden blonde hair falls in glossy waves as it dances around her shoulders.

"Chelsea," I acknowledge her, my voice horse. I shift my weight to adjust to the stiff, uncomfortable sling cradling my fractured shoulder, fighting to suppress the wince threatening to break through my facade of calm. "Appreciate the lift."

Her bright blue eyes gleam like polished sapphires. "Of course, Jack. Don't even mention it. We're friends, after all." She closes the gap between us, her perfume filling the air. It's intoxicatingly sweet, like sugar-spun carnivals, overpowering the lingering scent of spring blossoms.

"No strings, right?" I remind her as she steps into my personal space.

Her smile widens, becoming even more foxlike. She's too damn far into my personal space now. Her long, manicured fingers trace the rough edges of my sling.

"Don't be like that Jack. I mean one or two small strings couldn't hurt," she purrs. She titters, the sound sharp and jarring. Its crystal clear she doesn't intend on just giving me a ride home despite swearing on her grandmother's grave this would be a strictly platonic favor.

Exhaling a sigh, I step back putting much-needed distance between us. "Chelsea, we've been over this." I pause to gesture between us with my good hand. "This thing, whatever it was between us, is dead. It died a long time ago." I sigh. "Right now, I just need to focus on my health, and getting back on the field." The pulsating ache in my groin screams but not out of attraction to Chelsea. "Sex is the furthest thing from my mind right now. You understand that, right?"

At least not sex with you.

A flicker of disappointment passes over her features before she schools it back into a playful smile.

"Fine, it's your loss," she quips, spinning on her heel to stride around to the passenger's side of her car.

She pops open the door for me, her heels clicking against the asphalt as she sways back to her side.

With careful precision, I lower myself into the plush leather seat, trying to repress the grimace as pain blooms from my injured shoulder and bruised groin. Chelsea slides into the driver's seat, her lips forming a petulant pout. But at this point, I can't muster the energy to care. I fill my mind with thoughts of my recovery, football, and whether or not a certain opinionated physiotherapist will agree to help me out by taking me on as a client.

I click the seatbelt in place, positioning my sling over it as I resign myself to the strained silence that has settled in the car. Chelsea is a hot cheerleader with very few visible insecurities, she'll be fine. So, her little temper tantrum right now shall pass. Hopefully, onto another willing participant.

CHAPTER 5

KAMILLA

The day has been surprisingly smooth, outside of the little hiccup in my status quo that was Jackson. I finally get a few minutes to myself between clients and was about to make a coffee run to the pantry when Luis's annoying face flashes me a warm smile from the other side of the glass doors of the clinic. I swallow a sigh as he steps through, eyes crinkling at me.

"Hey sis," he greets me, his strong arms wrapping around me in a tight embrace. "Just thought I'd drop by and apologize for how I acted earlier."

"Huh-huh," I reply, returning his embrace before pulling back. Luis would never drive all the way to my clinic just to tell me he's sorry. Especially not for poking his nose in my business so something is definitely up. "We both know that's bullshit, though I will accept your fake apology. So, have at it, then spill the real reason you're here."

Luis runs a hand through his thick black hair, hesitating a moment. "Alright, you got me, I did want to talk -"

"Nope," I say, cutting him off. "You said you came here to offer an apology so, I'mma hold you to that before we go into anything else."

Luis shifts from one foot to another. "Fine, Kam. I acted out of character earlier and I'm sorry."

"Not good enough," I tease. "You can do better than that. What are you sorry for?"

Luis scowls at me and I widen my eyes, before dropping back onto the waiting room bench.

"Tick tock," I tease again.

Luis sighs. "I'm sorry, okay? You're my only sister and I worry about you. So, sometimes I get too deep into the nitty gritty when I think you're heading down a dark path. I know I can be a lot to deal with, and for that, I'm genuinely sorry."

"Homerun. Apology accepted," I say with a giggle. "So, what really brought you in here so late in the afternoon?"

Luis dropped onto the bench beside me with yet another sigh. "I need to talk to you about your services. You know, physio-therapy and all that."

My eyebrows rise at this unexpected turn of conversation. "What about it?"

Luis's gaze looks everywhere but at me. "Well, I was thinking about a teammate of mine. He's been having some trouble lately with an injury, and I thought maybe you could help him out."

My mood falls. "Please tell me you aren't talking about Jackson."

Luis meets my gaze for a beat before switching back to study the floor. "Come on, Kam. He needs us ... well you, right now."

"Like hell he does," I say, louder than intended as I spring to my feet. "I don't know what to tell you. But you wasted your time coming here. I'm already at my wit's end with him at home. Now you want me to deal with his disrespectful ass here too?" I blow out a breath. "Sorry, but no."

Luis stands to meet my eyes. "Come on, I know you hate him, but he may not be able to play again without your help."

I sigh. What I want to ask is now if that somehow becomes my problem but instead, I pull in a breath. "What did the doctor say was wrong with him?"

"Jackson didn't go into detail," Luis admits.

"Did he at least say what the doctor wanted me to do? What was his recommended treatment plan?" I ask, annoyed that not only did Jackson not have the balls to speak to me himself but he didn't even send full details.

"Nothing major, really," Luis replies, rubbing the back of his neck. "Just some sessions to help regain his strength and mobility. I think with your help he'll be back on the field in time for finals. "

"Is that so?" I ask, keeping my tone level. Jackson can be quite difficult and stubborn. There's very little confidence in my mind that Jackson will put his ego aside long enough to listen to any of my instructions.

"Look," Luis adds, catching the hesitation in my eyes, "I know you guys have your qualms, but Jackson really needs your help. I wouldn't ask if I didn't think you were his best chance at recovery. Plus, he assured me he'll lay off of making living with him hellish for you."

I let out a sigh, weighing my options. On one hand, helping someone like Jackson could further boost my reputation and prove my skills at a national level to those who doubt me. I'm pretty respected in my field locally but having a high-profile client like Jackson on my roster could help me spread my reach. On the other hand, though, being that close to Jackson, seeing him in such a vulnerable state may mess up the priorities in my head. Jackson may be pigheaded by he is also sexy as all get out and a massive tease.

"Here's an idea," Luis says, breaking my mind cycle. "You said you didn't want him messing up your safe space here in the clinic. I can totally get that. But y'all already live together." He pauses to study the confused look on my face. "What if you just did the therapy sessions there?"

I open my mouth to protest.

"Hear me out," Luis pushes back before I could speak. "It would be a win-win. You wouldn't have to deal with Jackson here in your one remaining safe space, and Jackson wouldn't have to bug people to transport him to and from the clinic." Luis meets my eyes. "Admit it, it could work."

I hesitate, my heart pounding as I wrap my mind around the idea. "I don't know, Luis. There are risks and complications involved with working outside of the clinic."

Like there being beds, condoms, and sex toys very close to our disposal. I think to myself.

An image of Jackson's smug face, leaning against my bedroom door in nothing but boxers telling me he's ready for our session flashes in my mind. I bite my lip, weighing my brother's words. Luis looks up at me with stupid puppy dog eyes and I sigh.

"Fine," I say finally, offering him a small smile. "I'll help him. But you better ensure he maintains his end of the bargain and cools down on his antics at home or I'mma move into your prized bachelor pad and send you to live with him."

Luis grins. his face lighting up. "He'll behave. You'll see."

We'll see about that.

Luis turns to leave.

"He better. Your apartment depends on it."

As Luis strides out of my office, I stare at the closed door, my mind a whirlwind of thoughts spiraling like a tempest in a teacup. I grab my phone from the bench, thumb hovering over the familiar chat icon labeled 'Sisterhood'. Sucking in a breath, I tap the icon, needing my refuge from reality.

Me:

Hey, ladies.

THE FRANTIC TAPPING of my fingers on the screen mirrors my heartbeat.

Me:
Guess who's about to become the physical therapist of the town's star quarterback.

THE RESPONSE IS IMMEDIATE, their replies tumbling over each other like pebbles in a stream. Trina's message pops up first, her words appearing on the screen with what I know to be pure astonishment.

TRINA:
Wait, what?
You're going to be Jackson Taylor's PT?
Like the roommate you can't stand, Jackson?
The annoying one?

Me:
That's the one.

LATALIA, never one to mince words, chips in next, her comment a stream of laughing emojis and biting humor.

. . .

LATALIA:

Does this call for a moment of silence?
Good luck dealing with that inflated ego.

LAUGHING I RESPOND.

Me:
I swear I can't with you, Tals.

NATASHA:

I think it could actually be a great opportunity for you, Kam.
Plus, it's a great way to put him in his place.

A CHUCKLE ESCAPES my lips at Natasha's optimism. She is ever the soothing voice of reason in our motley group. I appreciate her faith in me, and her belief that I can turn this predicament into an opportunity. But the thought of working so closely with Jackson makes my stomach churn.

As if sensing my dilemma, my phone buzzes again, breaking my chain of thoughts. but this time it's not from the Sisterhood. The message is from the one and only Sophia Martinez - my workmate turned friend, her long black hair and huge brown eyes as familiar to me as my own reflection. Her warmth, friendliness, and ability to make friends effortlessly have always drawn people to her. She is, in a way, the soothing balm to my fiery nature in this sometimes-miserable clinic.

. . .

SOPHIA:

Just heard the news from your brother on his way out.
How do you feel about it?

I PULL IN A BREATH. *Damn you, Luis.* I'm yet to fully wrap my mind around the idea yet, and he's already out there spreading the news.

Me:
To be honest, I don't know, Soph.
I guess I'm still wrapping my head around it. It's a great professional
opportunity.
But the idea of working so closely with Jackson... It's daunting.

HER REPLY IS swift and comforting.

SOPHIA:

Just keep in mind that he's the one who needs you in this scenario.
Not the other way around.

THOSE WORDS, so simple yet profound, act as a lighthouse guiding me through a storm of emotions. Sophia's right. Maybe I've been looking at this all wrong. This isn't about Jackson, or his antics, or my complicated feelings towards him. It's about my career, my journey, and the mark I intend to leave in an industry that's been nothing but skeptical of me.

Me:
Thank you.

SOPHIA:

Always here for you, girl.
I hear there's a fresh brew in the pantry. Coffee run?

I SMILE.

Me:
I'm actually about to head out, but I'll take a rain check.

WITH ALL THE thoughts in my head finally settling, I click back
into the Sisterhood chat.

Me:
I can't believe I'm about to say this but... I think I can handle Jackson
Taylor.

TRINA:

Think? Girl, of course, you can. Wanna know why?

TRINA, Latalia, Natasha, and I all message the answer at virtually
the same time.

. . .

Me:
Cause I'm a badass B who refuses to take shit while finding success and
taking names.

I LAUGH to myself as I promise to holla at them later, tuck my phone in my pocket, and head out to my car to drive home.

The ride home is somewhat peaceful. Well as peaceful as it can be in city traffic. But the peace fades the moment I step into my apartment. My bedroom doorknob is visible from the front doorway, and a pair of scandalous black lace panties hang from it like a banner of disgrace, taunting me. My lungs collapse in on themselves trying to expel the disappointment that's stuck inside me—a reminder that no matter how hard I try Jackson will always be an ass.

"Stupid," I mutter under my breath, gritting my teeth. My hands ball into fists as I march to my room door and snatch the ratchet pair of panties.

"Jackson!" I shout, storming down the hallway toward his room. I didn't sign up for this when I became his roommate. The door is wide open, and I find him lying on his bed, pretending to flip through a sports magazine. He looks up, surprise flickering across his handsome face, followed by a sharp intake of breath and an animalistic groan before I can rip him a new one.

Jackson winces, clutching his arm tightly against his chest while trying to hide the pain in his eyes.

"Fucking hell," he hisses under his breath, beads of sweat forming on his forehead.

As much as I'd like to tell him where to shove these panties, I can't. Not with the pang of guilt filling my gut. He might be a jerk, but he's also human, and clearly in need of help. I sigh, my gaze fixed on his pained expression.

"Are you alright?" I ask, even though I know the answer.

"Peachy," he grits out, his jaw clenched. "Just a little sore."

"Little?" I scoff, crossing my arms. "You look like you're about to pass out."

"Thanks for the vote of confidence," he grumbles, shooting me a glare. But then, his gaze falls on the black lace panties still in my hand, and his expression softens. "Look, Kamilla, I'm sorry about the panties. It was a stupid prank. I knew you were upset about the one on the Espresso machine earlier and I thought it would've been funny. I shouldn't have done it."

"Damn right, you shouldn't have," I retort, my anger refusing to dissipate. "But that doesn't change the fact that you're hurt and need help."

A flicker of vulnerability crosses his face, but he quickly masks it with a forced smile. "Yeah. Thanks for agreeing to help me with my physiotherapy."

I nod, tossing the panties onto his bed. "Don't expect me to coddle you. Knowing you, you brought this on yourself."

"Understood," he says, his voice strained as he cradles his arm. There's a brief moment of tension-filled silence between us with an undercurrent of something I can't quite place.

I sigh. "Get some rest." I turn to leave his room. "Your first session starts early tomorrow morning at 5 AM."

"5 AM?" he asks, his jaw-dropping open ever so slightly.

"Yep," I nod, forcing an icy tone. "Bright and early. Don't be late."

"Wouldn't dream of it," he replies, his eyes twinkling with that familiar mischief.

My thoughts race as I head for my own room. I'm angry, but there's also an undeniable thrill in knowing I have the power to help Jackson heal – or make him suffer. And while I might hate him, I am looking forward to seeing him in nothing but boxers or better yet a towel.

"God, get a grip, Kamilla," I chastise myself, shaking off the unwelcome fantasies. "Jackson is, now and forever will be, just a roommate. And a client. And I hate him... Right?"

CHAPTER 6

JACKSON

I step into the living room and a wave of lavender assaults my senses. Soft instrumental music plays in the background, the lights dimmed. My shoulders grow tense.

Kamilla stands by the mat in the center of the room, her dark wavy hair pulled into a loose bun, wearing those damn yoga pants that cling to her curves and a sports bra that leaves little to the imagination. She turns, icy brown eyes assessing me with a clinical detachment that makes my skin prickle.

"On the mat, Jackson. We have a lot of work to do." Her tone is crisp and professional as if she's talking to any other patient and not the man she's lived with for almost a year. The woman infuriates me.

I swallow a retort and make my way over, shrugging off my shirt. No point in arguing when she's in one of her moods. My shoulder aches, bruises still mottling my skin. I lower myself to the mat, gritting my teeth against the flare of pain.

Kamilla crouches beside me, gently probing the joint. Her

touch is surprisingly tender and heat pools low in my gut. I clench my jaw, staring at the far wall.

"The swelling has gone down, but there's significant damage to the tendons and ligaments. This will be an intensive recovery process, Jackson." Her voice softens. "I know we haven't seen eye to eye recently, but I need you to trust me. Can you do that?"

I risk a glance at her. For a moment, I glimpse the caring yet infuriating woman I can't get out of my head far behind those damned professional walls. My breath catches and I nod.

A smile curves her lips. "Good. Now, take a deep breath and relax. We have a long road ahead."

Her hands begin to work their magic, easing the tension in my muscles. I close my eyes, the scent of lavender and Kamilla surrounding me, and for the first time in weeks, an unfamiliar peace settles over me. Maybe this whole physiotherapy thing won't be so bad after all.

Kamilla's fingers dig into the knotted muscles of my shoulder, and I wince.

"Sorry," she murmurs. "I have to work out these adhesions before we can properly assess your range of motion."

I grit my teeth against the pain, determined not to make a sound. She won't get the satisfaction of seeing me squirm.

Her hands pause. "Relax, Jackson. Tensing up will only make it worse."

I force myself to take a deep breath and release the tension in my body. To my surprise, the pain lessens.

Kamilla's hands resume their ministrations, gently coaxing my muscles into submission. A groan rumbles in my chest before I can stop it.

"There, you see?" Amusement colors her voice. "Isn't that better?"

"Just get on with it," I mutter. I won't give her the pleasure of a proper response.

She sighs. "Why must you always make things so difficult?"

Her fingers dig in with renewed force and I jerk. "Relax. Breathe. Let go of this ridiculous tension between us so we can move forward."

I glare at her. "You're the one who started this whole thing. If you haven't noticed, we're not exactly on the best of terms lately."

She scoffs. "Me? And whose fault is that Cassanova?" She prods my shoulder sharply. "You've been insufferable since I moved in. I'm trying to extend an olive branch here by helping you. The sooner we move past whatever this is, the sooner your joints will heal, and we can go our separate ways."

Go our separate ways. The words hit me like a blow to the gut. When did everything get so screwed up? I swallow hard, staring up at the ceiling.

"You're right," I whisper. "I'm sorry. Can we call a truce for today?"

With her hands still on my shoulder, she gives it a gentle squeeze. "I'd like that."

She resumes her assessment and I relax into her touch, the tension seeping out of my muscles. Her fingers knead into my shoulder, finding each knot and releasing it with practiced ease. A groan slips out before I can stop it and heat floods my cheeks.

Kamilla's breath hitches. Her hands still again, resting on my bare skin, and the air between us grows charged. I dare a glance at her from under my lashes and find her already watching me, eyes dark and unreadable.

The moment stretches on, neither of us moving. I swallow hard as a rush of awareness washes over me, hyper-aware of each point of contact between us. My skin tingles under her touch and I fight the urge to arch into her hands, to pull her closer.

What the hell is wrong with me? This is Kamilla, for God's sake. The same woman I promised Luis I'd stay away from.

I jerk away from her, clearing my throat. "I think that's enough for now."

Hurt flashes across her face before she schools her features into a neutral mask. She nods briskly, gathering up her supplies. "Fine. Get plenty of rest and keep icing your shoulder. We can resume our session later tonight but in the spirit of being cordial, how about I cook us dinner when I get back from work?"

"That would be nice," I admit.

Kamilla nods and then sweeps from the room without another word, leaving me alone with the memory of her touch and a mess of confusing thoughts I don't know what to do with. I rake my good hand through my hair and sigh.

This whole situation just got a hell of a lot more complicated.

I spend the rest of the day avoiding Kamilla, holed up in my room, and trying to distract myself. But my thoughts keep drifting back to our session this morning, the feel of her hands on my skin and the awareness that had sparked between us.

I don't know what the hell is going on, but I need to get a grip. Kamilla is off-limits, no matter what kind of crazy chemistry we seem to have. She's my roommate, my physiotherapist, and the sister of my best friend. Nothing more. I intend to keep my promise.

Even if it kills me.

By the time Kamilla knocks on my door to call me for dinner, I've managed to convince myself that whatever I thought I'd felt between us earlier was all in my head. I paste on a smile and join her in the kitchen, determined to act normal. We eat in silence at first, the tension in the room so thick you could cut it with a knife. I clear my throat, searching for something casual to say.

"So, how was the rest of your day?" I ask.

Kamilla shrugs, not meeting my eyes. "Fine. Yours?"

"Good, just relaxing. Getting ready for our next session tomorrow." I try for a teasing grin. "Wouldn't want you going easy on me out of pity."

She looks up at that, a spark of challenge entering her gaze. "Don't worry, I won't." A hint of a smile plays at the corner of her mouth. "As I said earlier, Cassanova, we still have a lot of work left to do. Speaking of, ready to jump back in?"

"Why not," I say, relief washing over me as the tension eases between us, our usual banter falling into place. By the time we finish dinner, things feel almost back to normal. Maybe I really did imagine that moment of awareness between us. Maybe this whole attraction I seem to have developed will fade in time.

I just have to keep telling myself that Kamilla is off-limits. No matter what.

Kamilla stands to set up what looked to be electrotherapy equipment, directing me to lie face down on the mat. I settle in, acutely aware of her movements around me.

She places one hand on my lower back, sending a jolt of warmth through me. "Ready?"

I swallow hard. "As I'll ever be."

The first pulses of electricity course through my shoulder, making my muscles twitch. Kamilla keeps her hand firmly in place, grounding me as the sensations intensify.

"How's the pain level?" Her voice is soft and intimate. "We want to push your limits but not go too far."

I grit my teeth against the discomfort, focusing on her touch. "I can handle it."

"I know you can." Her thumb rubs small circles on my back, both soothing and igniting my nerves. "But there's no need to prove anything here. I'm in control of the intensity, so just tell me if it's too much."

The implication of her words hits me, arousal stirring low in my belly. I'm helpless under her ministrations, at the mercy of her hands, and I find I don't entirely mind.

The session passes in a haze of electricity and touch. By the time Kamilla removes the electrodes, a dull ache has settled into my shoulder but the rest of me feels hypersensitive.

I sit up, catching her gaze. There's that awareness again that makes my pulse quicken, but she busies herself with packing up the equipment.

"We'll do some light exercises next time," she says, her voice a bit rushed. "But we'll also be moving our focus to the groin. So, keep up with the icing, and let me know if there's more pain than usual."

"I will." I stand on unsteady legs, hesitating. "Thanks, Kamilla. For...you know. Helping me."

She nods. "You're welcome. Just doing my job."

I leave the room in a daze, haunted by her touch. So much for convincing myself this attraction would fade, if anything, it's only getting stronger. And that scares the hell out of me.

CHAPTER 7

KAMILLA

The last 2 days have been torture. The air between me and Jackson has shifted somehow, and I can't tell if it's for the better or not. I almost wish he was still being an ass as until his scheduled session he'd been avoiding me like I had a plague. Now with nowhere to hide the awkwardness is on high. I stand between Jackson's legs, my hands on his thighs as I explain the intricate connections between his leg joints and muscles.

"You see, the adductor muscles here connect to your groin, which can cause strain and discomfort if not properly stretched," I explain.

My heart races, the proximity of our bodies making it difficult to focus. Jackson sits there, clad in only his boxers, and a surge of attraction surges through me despite our antagonistic relationship. I swallow hard, trying to hide my inner turmoil.

"Okay," Jackson says, a hint of apprehension in his voice. "Just do whatever you need to do."

I massage his legs, and his reactions tell me the effect my

actions have on him. His breathing becomes heavier, his body tenses up, and an undeniable bulge forms in his boxers.

"Jackson," I say, struggling to maintain a professional tone. "Try to relax. This will help alleviate the pain."

"Right," he replies, gritting his teeth. "Relax. Got it."

Despite my efforts to remain detached, the heat radiating from his body pulls me into him as my fingers work their way up his thighs. I know I should keep an emotional distance, but it's becoming more difficult with every passing second.

"Kamilla," he breathes, his voice strained. "That feels... really good."

His tone is hungry, and his words send a shiver down my spine. I bite my lip to suppress a moan. It's like we're dancing on the edge of a precipice, one wrong step away from plummeting into the abyss of unspoken desire.

"Thank you," I stammer, forcing myself to concentrate on the massage. "It's important to keep your muscles loose and limber."

But as I continue massaging up to his groin area, the tension between us becomes palpable. His arousal is evident and pulsing, and I'd be lying to say it wasn't distracting as all hell.

"Kamilla," Jackson whispers, his eyes locked onto mine. "I don't know if I can handle this."

"Jackson, we're both adults," I remind him, trying to ignore the pounding in my chest as his bulge pulses. "It's just a physio-therapy session, we can get through this. Just focus on your breathing and let me do my job."

Drawing in a breath, I work my hands over his strained muscles, the heat of his arousal evident beneath my fingertips as I continue to massage Jackson's leg. I inch closer to his groin, and the tension between us reaches a breaking point. His blue eyes lock onto mine, and an electric current pass through our gaze. The silence in the room is heavy, charged with suppressed desires that we both know we can't act on.

"Kamilla," he murmurs again, his voice barely audible, as if he's afraid of shattering the fragile balance we've managed to maintain so far.

"Jackson," I reply, my voice equally hushed. My fingers move expertly over his muscles, keeping up the pretense of professionalism. Inside, though, I'm a mess of conflicting emotions. I hate him for making me feel this way, but at the same time, the magnetic pull between us grows stronger and stronger.

"Your, uh... your technique is really effective," he stammers, trying to steer the conversation back to safer ground.

"Thank you," I say, forcing myself to focus on the physiological aspects of the massage. "The adductor muscles play a vital role in stabilizing the pelvis and supporting the hip joint."

But even as I recite the facts, my mind betrays me with thoughts of straddling his bare dick. The temptation to explore further is almost overwhelming.

"Your muscles are really tense here," I say, my voice wavering as I realize the double meaning of my words. "It's important to release this tension to avoid any imbalances or injuries."

"Right," he replies, his breathing growing heavier. It's clear that he's struggling to keep his arousal in check, just as I am.

"Kamilla, I..." he begins, but then seems to lose his nerve. Instead, he swallows hard and asks, "Is there anything else I should be doing to help with my recovery?"

"Stretching and strengthening exercises are crucial," I say, grateful for the opportunity to focus on something more clinical. "I can show you a few that will target the specific areas we're working on."

"Okay," he agrees, nodding his head as if trying to force himself to concentrate on what I'm saying.

But as our eyes meet once more, I swear my own need is mirrored in his eyes.

I can't ignore it any longer. Jackson's erection is impossible to overlook, straining against his boxers as he shifts uncomfortably on the couch. My own arousal is equally undeniable, heat pooling at my core as our eyes meet.

"Jackson," I say hesitantly, swallowing hard. "Maybe you should... remove your boxers. It might be more comfortable for you."

"Is that really necessary?" he asks, eyebrows raised, his voice strained from the effort of remaining composed.

"Look," I sigh, trying to convince myself this is about professionalism and not the fantasies swimming in my head. "We're both adults here, so let's just focus on your comfort. It will make the rest of the session easier."

He hesitates for a moment before nodding, his jaw clenched. He stands and peels off his boxers at a painfully slow pace. His throbbing dick pops free in all its glory. I will myself to look away, but my eyes lock in place, my pulse quickening.

Holy cock basket.

I swallow.

"Alright," I say, forcing myself to focus on the task at hand. "Let's continue."

Nodding, he sits on the couch.

My hands tremble as I place them back on his inner thigh, once again inching closer to his pulsing erection. My eyes flicker to its slick head and I drop them back to his legs.

Why did I suggest he take off his boxers?

With each passing second, the urge to touch him grows stronger. It's like his dick is calling to me, consuming my every thought.

I hate Jackson, remember?

Jackson has been an ass to me since I moved in here.

But I don't need to like him to fuck him, do I?

I swallow.

"Kamilla," Jackson whispers, his breath hitching as I brush against him. "Please."

I glance up at him, our gazes locking, and something within

me snaps. Without another word, I give in to temptation, wrapping my hand around his pulsing dick, feeling the heat radiate from him. The moan that escapes his lips is equal parts relief and surrender, mirroring my own feelings.

"God, Kamilla," he groans, his fingers digging into the couch cushions.

"Should I stop?" I ask, my voice wavering as I stroke him.

I know what we're doing is wrong – that it's playing with fire – but the thrill of crossing this forbidden line makes my heart race. My strokes become more deliberate, fueled by a curiosity I can no longer deny.

"Kamilla, I don't think I can hold on much longer," Jackson whispers through gritted teeth, his eyes clouded.

"Then don't," I whisper, my own resolve crumbling as I strengthen my strokes.

This doesn't have to mean anything, I tell myself. *It's just a moment of weakness between enemies.*

Deep down, I know I'm lying to myself. But there's something between us that I can't ignore, an attraction that won't be silenced until I explore this.

My grip tightens and Jackson gasps as the intensity increases.

"I need to relieve the tension in your groin area," I explain, desperately trying to maintain a facade of professionalism as I study him.

"Kamilla..." he groans, his voice filled with both pleasure and caution. His eyes lock onto mine.

"Relax, Jackson," I murmur, my hand gliding up and down his throbbing length in a steady rhythm. "Let me help you release."

I focus on the feeling of him in my hand, the velvety smoothness of his skin and the strong, steady pulse beneath it. The sounds of our heavy breathing and muffled moans mingle in the air, creating a symphony of desire that only heightens my own arousal.

"Fuck, Kamilla... If you keep doing that, I'm not going to last much longer," he pants, his fingers gripping the couch cushions so tightly that his knuckles turn white.

His vulnerability is intoxicating. I want to push him further, to explore the depths of this forbidden attraction.

"Then let go," I whisper as I intensify my strokes.

In this moment, there is no rivalry, no animosity—only the raw, carnal desire that courses through our bodies like a raging river.

"God, you're amazing," he rasps, his head falling back against the couch, his chest heaving with each ragged breath. I can't tear my gaze away from him, mesmerized by the sight of this strong, confident man brought to the edge by my touch.

"You have no idea how good this feels," he admits, his eyes dark with lust as they meet mine. The intensity of his gaze sends a shiver down my spine.

"Neither do you," I confess, the raw honesty in my voice startling even myself.

My thumb circles the sensitive head of his dick, eliciting a deep, throaty moan from him that spikes my arousal.

His breathing grows heavier, and moans fill the room.

"Fuck, I'm close," he pants, his body tensing as he teeters on the brink of release.

There's no turning back now. We've crossed a line that can't be uncrossed, and only time will tell if we'll survive the consequences.

"Cum for me, Jackson," I urge him, my voice barely more than a breathless whisper. "Get outta your mind and let go."

A bead of precum forms at the tip of his dick, and without thinking, I moisten my fingers with it and bring it to my mouth.

A moan escapes my lips and I bite down on my bottom lips to stay quiet. I return my now wet fingers to Jackson's dick, the taste of him still lingering on my tongue.

"God, Kami—" he starts to say, but I cut him off.

"Shut up and enjoy it while it lasts," I demand, increasing the pressure of my strokes, causing him to gasp and moan.

I stroke him faster, my eyes locked on him as he nods.

"Just like that," he groans, "Fuck, just like fucking that."

His breath quickens once more the veins on his dick pulsing and hard. Cum spills all over my hands as Jackson releases a guttural moan. The intensity of it all drives me wild with desire, but I know that this brief encounter cannot continue.

Guilt gnaws at my conscience as the adrenaline fades.

What have I done?

I swallow, refusing to meet Jackson's eyes. Standing I move over to the kitchen island and grab the container of wipes and hand it to Jackson, still looking everywhere but directly at him.

"You okay?" Jackson asks, his voice laced with concern. It's so unlike him that it startles me.

"Y-yeah," I stammer, trying to regain my composure. "I... I think we should end the session here for today."

"Alright," he replies, his tone hesitant.

Conflicted, I retreat to my bedroom, sinking into a pit of guilt as I question my choices. How could I have allowed myself to cross that line with Jackson? And worse, how can I deny that despite everything, a part of me still craves more?

"Damn you, Jackson Taylor," I whisper, burying my face in my pillow, knowing that things between us will never be the same again.

CHAPTER 8

JACKSON

The silence in the kitchen the next morning presses on us like a dense fog. Kamilla and I sit at the kitchen island, picking at our sandwiches as if they're puzzles we can't quite solve. My thoughts keep drifting back to the hand job she gave me, the way her fingers curled around me with such teasing confidence. As much as she wants me to believe it, I know it hadn't been part of my treatment, but I need to hear her say it.

"Kamilla," I say hesitantly, trying not to choke on my sandwich, "about what happened yesterday... That wasn't part of the physiotherapy, was it?"

Her eyes dart away from mine, and I see her cheeks flush a deep shade of brown. She swallows hard before shaking her head.

'No, Jackson, it wasn't."

My heart races, the tension between us crackling like electricity. I watch her fingers trail along the edge of her plate, the same fingers that mere hours ago brought me to the brink of pleasure.

"Then... why did you?" I ask, my voice barely above a whisper.

She hesitates, still avoiding my gaze. When she finally speaks, her voice is quiet, almost brittle.

She shrugs. "Truth?"

"Please," I say, willing her to meet my eyes.

"I wanted to," she admits. "It pains me to admit this as I would hate to further swell that inflated ego of yours. But for some reason I find you attractive."

Shock and confusion wash over me as I try to process Kamilla's words. I've done everything I could think of to stop her from having feelings for me.

"This doesn't need to change anything between us," she adds cutting my thoughts.

If I didn't know better, I'd swear there was a hint of disappointment in her voice.

"If we were to do this," I start, my voice wavering slightly with uncertainty, "I think it's important that we keep things physical. No emotions involved."

HER EYES FINALLY MEET MINE, relief flooding her features. "That I can do." She smiles, a genuine, warm smile that reaches her eyes. "We can fuck. No strings attached, no feelings getting in the way. Just satisfying our desires."

My chest tightens as I nod in agreement, knowing deep down that this arrangement may be harder to follow than either of us admits. But the alternative - opening up emotionally is something I'm not under any circumstances willing to explore. For now, keeping our connection purely physical seems like the safest option.

"So, we're on the same page then?" I ask, seeking confirmation as I reach for another bite of my sandwich.

"Definitely," she replies, her gaze steady and confident. "It's just about having fun, right?"

"Right," I echo, though the knot in my stomach tells me otherwise. It's hard to ignore the lingering glances, the subtle shifts in body language that betray more than just physical attraction.

"Alright," I agree, extending my hand to her. "Deal?"

"Deal," she replies, shaking my hand with a firm grip. Her touch sends a shiver down my spine, and I pull my hand away.

Turning my focus back on my food, I address the elephant in the room.

"We...we need to keep this a secret from Luis. You know how he is – protective, especially when it comes to you. He's my best friend, and I don't want anything to come between us."

"Agreed," she says, nodding her head. "Luis doesn't need to know about our arrangement. It's just between us." There's a sense of finality in her words, and I know that she understands the importance of keeping our secret.

"Besides," I add, trying to lighten the mood, "it's not like we're doing anything wrong. We're both consenting adults who've agreed to have some fun together. No harm, no foul."

"Exactly," she replies, offering me a small smile. "Nothing outside of sex will change between us, Jackson. We'll still be roommates; we won't need to hang out or do anything outside of what we usually do. This is just...a bonus."

"Right," I say, feeling a knot of tension in my chest begin to loosen. "Just a bonus."

WE FALL SILENT, each taking a moment to process what we've just agreed upon. My mind races with thoughts of our future encounters.

"Promise me one thing," Kamilla says, her gaze locking onto mine. "Promise me that if, at any point, either one of us starts to feel like this is getting too complicated or too emotional, we'll talk about it. We'll be honest with each other."

"Done," I reply without hesitation.

"Good," she says, her expression softening. "Now, finish your sandwich. You're going to need your strength for this to work."

A grin spreads across my face as I take another bite, the anticipation of what's to come electrifying every nerve in my body.

Kamilla as she brushes a stray lock of hair behind her ear, the gesture both innocent and alluring.

"Let's set some ground rules," I suggest.

"Alright," Kamilla agrees, her brown eyes studying me. "What do you have in mind?"

"First, no kissing." The words leave my mouth before I can second-guess them. Kissing feels too intimate, too close to crossing the line between physical pleasure and emotional attachment. Kamilla nods in agreement, understanding the need for detachment.

"I'm good with that," she says, her voice steady. "What else?"

"Second, we can only be intimate when we're alone. Having others see us will only lead to complications.

Kamilla laughs.

"Did something about me scream exhibitionist?" she asks, her tone teasing. "We don't need any unnecessary drama in our lives. Anything else?"

"Nope, I guess we have an understanding," I say, extending my coffee cup. Kamilla clinks the cup with hers.

"Here's to keeping things casual," Kamilla murmurs, a hint of excitement lacing her words.

"Cheers to that," I reply.

"I have to run," Kamilla says sliding off her stool. "I need you to ensure you do the exercises I recommended." A hint of a smile kisses the sides of her lips. "Especially the ones for your groin."

"Yes ma'am," I tease. Smiling back at her. "I have to head out too. Coach wants me at practice today."

Kamilla's eyes grow wide. "You are nowhere near being ready for the green yet. I sent over a full re –"

Laughter bubbles in my gut cutting her off. "Calm down, Mother. I'm just dropping by to grab some play tapes. No intensive activity." I hold three fingers up in the air. "Scout's honor."

Kamilla rolls her eyes. "Trust me, you wouldn't want your mother having the thoughts I have about you."

That catches me by surprise. "And what thoughts are those?"

Kamilla winks in my direction. "Touch, murder, and everything in between." She laughs and slips into her room and reemerges with her clinic bag. "Need a ride to the field?"

"With someone who just admitted to having thoughts of murdering me?" I tease, stifling a laugh. "I think I'm good."

"Have it your way," she teases before slipping through the door.

This day has not at all started out how I thought it would, but I can't lie and say I'm not looking forward to where this arrangement will lead.

My phone vibrates against the cold surface of the island countertop, Luis's name dominating the display. Guilt whirls its way through my stomach, but I manage to lift the phone, masking my internal turmoil with a cheerful greeting.

"Hey, Luis," I greet, trying to sound as nonchalant as possible. "You're downstairs?"

"Yeah," Luis replies, the unmistakable sounds of the city echoing in the background. "You ready?"

"Sure, let me just grab my jacket."

The jacket lands in my hands after a brief search, and a quick "Sure" dropped into the phone before ending the call. I take a final glance at Kamilla's empty seat, the echo of our agreement still lingering in the air. With a deep breath, I push it from my mind, grab my jacket, and head downstairs.

Sliding into the passenger seat of Luis's car, unease wiggles its way into my thoughts. Guilt gnaws at my conscience, but I force a smile, greeting Luis with a fist bump.

As Luis navigates through the city's morning rush, Kamilla's image is rooted firmly in my thoughts. Seeing Luis right after agreeing to benefits with Kamilla is brutal. Our arrangement needs to remain a secret at all costs. Luis is a psycho when it comes to Kamilla. So, protecting this secret is not only for the sake of Kamilla and me but for the sake of the team's dynamic.

Once at the practice grounds, I grab the tapes from Coach before taking a seat on the bench. Observing from the sidelines has become a routine since my injury, yet this time the physical pain is shadowed by a deeper, emotional ache. Guilt courses through me once more, sharper than any physical injury, as Luis does an elaborate gesture, pointing to me after scoring a touch-down. I swallow.

Time stretches out, punctuated by the staccato of boots against the ball, the gruff commands of the coach, and the play-ers' grunts of effort. I keep my focus on the team, on Luis, my mind whirling with thoughts of what our new arrangement could mean for my friendship, for the team, for Kamilla. The secret becomes an unbearable weight, threatening to unseat my composure.

Luis's concern cuts through the tension as the practice ends, his voice pulling me back from the precipice of my spiraling thoughts.

"How are you holding up, man?"

I shrug, a feeble smile attempting to mask the internal tumult.

"It's still weird not being out there with all of you," I admit, hoping my voice doesn't betray the turmoil within me. "Can't wait to get back in the game."

"You will," Luis says, slapping me on the shoulder making me flinch. "Sorry, man… habit. Just keep listening to Kamilla. She may be annoying, but she's good at what she does."

Oh, you have no idea how true that is.

But of course, I cannot say that.

"I'm trying," I say instead, the irony of his instructions not lost on me.

Luis smiles. "Good, cause we need you back on the green like yesterday." He sighs. "Let's get you outta here."

With a nod, I stand and join him, hoping like hell the ride back to the apartment can be done in silence.

CHAPTER 9

JACKSON

*M*y eyes flutter open and my nose twitches as the scent of bacon wafts into the room. Its rich and smoky aroma mingles with the earthy, robust fragrance of freshly brewed coffee. The delicious smells envelop me, stirring something deep within, a hunger that goes beyond mere sustenance.

I follow the enticing scents to the kitchen. There, Kamilla stands by the stove, cooking breakfast in one of her oversized t-shirts. It hangs off her shoulder, teasing me with a glimpse of her smooth, dark skin. The soft rhythm of a sultry song fills the air, and she sways to the beat. My eyes drop to her ass bouncing under the fabric and my cock hardens.

"Morning," I greet her, my voice husky. She turns her head toward me, a mischievous smile playing on her lips, her eyes sparkling.

"Good morning, Jackson," she replies, her voice sultry and inviting. "I hope you're hungry because I made plenty."

My eyes trail down her body as she turns to flip the bacon in the pan, each motion causing her shirt to ride up slightly, revealing a tantalizing sliver of her firm ass cheeks.

I swallow hard, my mouth growing dry as I struggle to focus on anything other than the way her hips move in time with the music.

"Starving," I admit, my voice barely more than a whisper.

Not for food though.

This is gonna be one hell of a morning.

The song changes and Kamilla's hips speed up to match the new beat.

I swallow a groan.

"Kamilla," I say, my voice far deeper than usual.

She looks over at me, her eyes alight with amusement. "Yes, Jackson?"

I take a step toward her, then another, feeling the magnetic pull between us grow stronger with each movement.

"You're driving me crazy; you know that?" I confess.

Her lips curl into a knowing smile, and a spark of mischief fills her eyes. "Am I now?"

"Undeniably," I reply, closing the distance between us until I'm standing right behind her.

I reach around her waist, my hands settling on the curve of her hips, feeling the heat of her body through the thin fabric of the shirt she's wearing. "But that is your intention. Isn't it?"

Kamilla leans back against me, her ass fitting perfectly against my now solid cock.

"I have no clue what you are on about," she murmurs, tilting her head back to look up at me. "But if it's working..."

She purrs. Fucking purrs, and it takes everything in me to not bend her over the counter next to the stove.

I nuzzle her neck, breathing in the intoxicating scent of her skin, mixed with the aroma of breakfast cooking. She shivers slightly at the contact, and her ass presses back further against my growing arousal.

"Keep wiggling your ass like that, and I'm going to end up fucking you right here on this counter."

Without skipping a beat, she grinds her ass further onto my cock, her movements deliberate and taunting. She switches off the stove, before tilting her head up, her eyes meeting mine with a mischievous glint.

"Is that a threat, Mr. Taylor?" she asks, her voice sultry and smooth.

"More like a promise," I respond, the pulse in my cock matching the pounding in my chest.

Kamilla smirks and bites her bottom lip, her gaze never leaving mine. The air around us crackles as my hands tighten on her waist.

Despite the intensity of this moment, I hesitate, unsure if I should give in to this maddening attraction or hold back. Sure, she's already jerked me off. But full-on fucking her, is a point we will never be able to come back from.

"Jackson," she breathes, her voice laced with desire, "I want this. But we need to make sure we're on the same page. This...whatever this is between us, it stays between us."

Her acknowledgment pushes me out of my head, and I drop my lips to her ear, sucking on her earlobe before traveling down to her neck."

Kamilla moans, her neck tilting to allow me access.

"I know you're doing this whole intimacy thing for me," Kamilla whispers, giving my chest a gentle push. "But fuck the foreplay. I need you now."

"RIGHT HERE?" I ask playfully, but with an unspoken seriousness that says this is no joke.

"Fuck yes," she growls, and that's all the confirmation I need.

I lift Kamilla onto the kitchen counter, ignoring her legs wrapping around my waist. My fingers trace the hem of her shirt, teasing the smooth, exposed skin beneath it before lifting it over her head and tossing it aside.

"God, you're beautiful," I whisper as I take in the sight of her. Her breasts are just perky enough to be perfect, nipples large and hard. My eyes roam over her full hips down to the glorious thin line of hair leading to her swollen clit.

"Is cooking with no panties a new habit, or have you always been out here bare and waiting?" I tease.

"Less talking, more fucking," Kamilla commands, her eyes darkening.

I grin and press my body against hers, my erection straining against my boxers, desperate for release. She moans as I grind against her, reaching down to relieve myself of my clothing. With a swift motion, I free my throbbing cock, and we both sigh in anticipation.

"Are you sure about this?" I ask, seeking one last moment of consent before diving into something we can't control.

"More than anything," she replies, her voice breathy. "I've been on the pill for years, and I know it's just a casual fuck. And I am very okay with that. Now, for the love of all things holy, put me outta my misery and fuck me."

Without another word, I position myself at her entrance, feeling the wetness of her arousal already coating me. With one final look into each other's eyes, I thrust forward, burying myself as far as her opening would allow.

Kamilla cries out at the connection, and I pull my cock back to the tip before thrusting back into her.

"Fuck, Kamilla," I groan, my hips already finding a steady rhythm as she clings to me, her nails digging into my shoulders. "You feel so fucking good."

I repeat the motion, each thrust deeper than before.

"Harder, Jackson," she demands, and I gladly comply.

The sound of flesh meeting flesh echoes throughout the kitchen, a steady rhythm that drives us both wild. Kamilla's moans mix with my own heavy breaths, creating a symphony of lust and desire.

"Fuck, Jackson, right there!" Kamilla gasps, the nails of her left hand digging into my shoulder as I thrust deeper inside her. The sensation of being so intimately connected with her is overwhelming, filling me with an intense heat that threatens to consume me.

"God, you feel amazing," I groan, unable to tear my eyes away from the sight of our bodies joining together. Sweat coats our skin, making it slick and welcoming to the touch, while the scent of our mingled arousal fills my nostrils. It's intoxicating, a heady reminder of just how badly I've wanted this.

"Harder," Kamilla demands, her words punctuated by forceful thrusts. "Please, Jackson, I need more."

"Anything for you, baby," I promise, complying with her request. My hands grip her hips, guiding her as our pace quickens, our movements growing more desperate and frantic with each passing moment.

Her eyes meet mine, a fiery passion burning within them, igniting something primal within me. "Don't stop, Jackson. Don't ever stop."

I dip my head to suck one of her nipples into my mouth eliciting a moan from Kamilla.

"Faster," Kamilla gasps, her body trembling beneath me, her pussy clenching against my cock telling me she's close.

I pound into her.

"Fucking cum for me, baby," I urge her, feeling my own climax building within me.

I drop my left hand down to her clit, rubbing the nub while pounding into her. Faster. Harder. Deeper.

With a scream of my name, Kamilla shatters around me, her pussy clenching tight onto my cock as her orgasm sends me over the edge. We ride out the waves of pleasure together, our bodies pulsing and shaking with the intensity of our release.

As we come down from our high, I rest my forehead against hers, our breaths mingling in the small space between us.

"I could get used to breakfasts like this," Kamilla teases, sliding down from the counter with a devilish smile.

"I bet," I tease, stepping back and then doubling over as a sharp pain shoots into my groin.

Kamilla grips my hips. "Fuck, are you okay?"

"Yeah," I lie, ignoring the growing pain as I straighten.

The last thing I need is for Kamilla to feel guilty in any way right now, as I loved every minute of that and would hate to have her second-guessing ever doing it again.

Kamilla glares at me. "Don't lie to me. I can see you're in pain. Is it your groin or shoulder?"

I sigh. "A little of both."

"I'm so fucking stupid," she curses herself under her breath.

My gut falls. "You're not stupid."

"Yeah well, I knew better. And having you do all that activity wasn't a smart decision for your recovery." She sighs. "Regardless of how good it felt."

She moves to grab something from her bedroom, and I pull on my boxers before moving to sit on the couch.

She returns with two heating pads and bends in front of me to pull them in, her body still on full display.

I grip her around her waist, ignoring the sting in my shoulder as I pull her into me and plant a kiss on her navel, the lingering scent of our mixed juices sending me into a frenzy.

"I have zero regrets about sleeping with you," I say pulling back to look up at her.

She doesn't respond, instead, she sets one of the heating pads on my shoulder and stoops to position the other on my groin.

"Kamilla," I say, my voice firm. "Look at me."

She shifts to her knees before meeting my eyes. The horror in them rips me up inside. I hate that she is in her head about this. About us.

I don't think, as I pull her into me, my hands gripping her shoulders as I lower my head to meet hers and capture her lips with mine. Our kiss is slow and passionate; our tongues slipping and mingling in a way that sends shivers down my spine. I caress her cheeks softly as our mouths continue to explore, our breathing growing heavier by the second.

Kamilla moans against my lips, climbing up into the chair to straddle me without resting her body on my legs. It's all the invitation I need to deepen the kiss. I slide one hand around her back while sliding the other up into her hair, gripping it tightly as the kiss becomes more frantic and desperate.

Her nipples press into my chest as I pull her into me, pouring out all I which I could say but can't into the kiss. Kamilla runs her hands over my back, caressing me until eventually I pull back. She gazes up at me with an intensity I've never seen from her before, before leaning forward to plant a light kiss on my neck.

"Thank you," she whispers against my ear.

I smile, as she shifts to sit on the couch. I stroke her hair and hold her close, an overwhelming sense of peace filling me that I know I have no business feeling.

Kamilla clears her throat, pulling free. "We should eat, and I need to get ready for work."

"Of course," I say, ignoring the pang of disappointment from the loss of her close to me.

She moves to the kitchen to fix us both plates and pours out two mugs of coffee.

"Keep the heating pad on for at least thirty minutes then try doing the light version of the exercises I showed you," she says handing me a plate before throwing back on her shirt.

I nod. The aura of intimacy that had been building fades just as quickly as it came.

"I won't be back until late today," she says avoiding my eyes.

"But I'm off from the clinic tomorrow. So, I'll be able to give you a more detailed assessment then."

I knew what I was in for when I agreed to casual hookups. Hell, casual is what I do, well did before Kamilla moved in. Yet, her sudden switch in demeanor leaves my head spinning as she grabs her plate and then disappears into her bedroom without another word.

I need to get a fucking grip.

CHAPTER 10

I didn't really need to work late yesterday. But I needed space from Jackson to clear my head. I know I can handle casual sex. I've done it before. Granted, I'm currently breaking damn near all my rules for friend-with-benefits situationships but I had hoped fucking Jackson would have gotten my stupid attraction to him out of my system, and I'd be able to continue our sessions without stupid fantasies interfering.

Boy was I wrong.

And it didn't help that he kissed me like his soul was meant to be with mine. I mean what in the heck was that?

I've hidden away in my room since getting home last night, but I can't hide forever.

Sighing, I zombie walk from my bedroom into the living room, my head throbbing from yet another vivid fantasy of riding and sucking Jackson's heavenly dick. The TV is on full blast with Jackson sprawled on the couch in front of it. I roll my eyes when I see it's a football rerun featuring Jackson.

"Really, Jackson?" I scoff, nudging him in a tease. "A little cocky, aren't we?"

He looks at me with a smirk, his green eyes sparkling with mischief. "You know as much as I do that those two words should never be in the same sentence when referring to me."

His eyebrows dance and I roll my eyes, a giggle bubbling in my gut.

"You're so full of yourself," I tease.

"I'd much rather be filling you," he retorts without missing a beat.

"God," I say, slapping him on his good shoulder. "Do you ever quit?"

He laughs. "Coach wants me to study the plays while I sit out for a few days as you suggested. He wants me to heal up before my check-in with the doc on Monday."

"Sure, sure," I say, not entirely convinced but decided to let it go. "How are your joints feeling today?"

"Much better thanks to those magical heating pads and light exercises you taught me," Jackson admits.

His admissions cut at some of the remaining guilt from yesterday's excursion.

"So, what brings you here on the couch alone?" I ask, my tone a light tease. "Don't you have any hot new cheerleaders to entertain you?"

My question is poised as a light tease, but deep inside a small part of me wants to know I've curved his sexual appetite.

Jackson raises an eyebrow, his grin widening. "Actually, I'd much rather spend the day with you," he says, making my stupid heart skip a beat. "I promise, I'll make you smile."

"Is that so?" I tease back, trying to hide my surprise and the warmth spreading through my chest. "If you're not careful, someone might think you actually like my company."

Jackson shrugs.

"Maybe I do," he replies, locking his eyes onto mine, and for a moment, the world around us disappears.

"Okay, then," I say, a sudden rush of boldness running through me. "Since we both have the day off, we could do something together? After yesterday, though wild counter sex is off the table. So, we may have to…" I pause to fake a shiver, "talk or something?"

I stifle a laugh.

"Sounds like a plan," he agrees, catching me off guard. He smiles up at me, with what I believe to be a genuine smile. "Let's do it."

"Let's whip up some breakfast before our day starts," I suggest, heading to the kitchen. Jackson follows suit and stands by the fridge before turning to me as I rummage through the cupboard for ingredients.

"How about an omelet with all the fixings?" Jackson suggests, grabbing eggs, onions, tomatoes, and bell peppers from the fridge. "Maybe I should cook for you today."

"Trying to poison me after just one hit?" I tease, causing Jackson to choke on laughter. "I've been living in this apartment for damn near eleven months and outside of your lady visitor's undies, I've seen no other proof you've even been near the kitchen."

Jackson looks up to the sky and then shrugs, laughing. "I can't even protest that one. How about we make it together?"

"I'm flattered, but how about you rest for now," I say, grabbing a cutting board. I chop the vegetables with precision. The colorful medley of red and green peppers, tomatoes, and onions becomes a rainbow on my board. Jackson, ever the charmer, offers his assistance once more, but I shoo him away, not wanting him to strain his injured arm any further on my behalf.

"Sit down and enjoy the show," I tease, switching on some

music. Jackson smiles, as an African beat fills the room. I wind my waist to the rhythm as I crack the eggs into a bowl.

Jackson climbs up on the other end of the counter to take a front-row seat, as my hips mirror the whisk as I combine the eggs with a little milk and seasoning. Dancing is in my blood. So, if putting on a show like I'd be doing anyway gets Jackson to rest his arm. So be it.

Swinging my hips, I heat butter in a non-stick pan, reviling in the sizzle as it melts. Adding the vegetables, I sauté them until they're just tender, then pour in the egg mixture, spreading it evenly across the pan. As the omelet cooks, I grate a generous amount of cheddar cheese over the top, still bubbling my hips.

"Looks amazing," Jackson says, his mouth-watering. "And not just the food."

"Wait till you taste it," I reply, grinning. I can do innuendos too. With a flick of my wrist, I fold the omelet in half, allowing the melted cheese to ooze out just a tad.

"Please tell me that can be on the menu today," Jackson whips back.

I smile, ignoring him as I slide the omelet onto a serving plate before splitting it in two with a fork.

"Silence means consent where I'm from," he presses again.

Once more, I remain silent, beckoning for him to follow me to the dining table. Jackson slips in across from me, but I avoid his eyes.

I scoop up a forkful of my omelet, the cheese melting and pulling apart in a mouthwatering display. Holding it out towards Jackson, I tease, "You really should dive in."

With a smirk, he leans in and nips the bite straight off my fork. "Mmm, this is divine," he says, eyes locked onto mine.

"Obviously. But I'm sure it tastes even better knowing you didn't have to lift a finger to make it," I quip, shooting him a cheeky grin.

His laughter fills the room. "Hey, I'll have you know I can

whip up a mean grilled cheese sandwich. That's gourmet in some places."

I can't hold back my laughter. "If grilled cheese is your version of gourmet, we seriously need to expand your horizons."

He pretends to stroke his chin in thought. "I'll consider it, but only if you promise to be my personal chef."

Raising an eyebrow, I retort, "Didn't you just offer to make me breakfast? How did I go from that offer to you flip-flopping to me being your chef? Make up your mind."

He leans closer, his chin resting on his good arm. His eyes are intense, piercing. "I'm only this indecisive when it comes to food. Everything else," his gaze roams over me, sending tingles down my spine, "I'm quite sure about."

Refusing to let him see he's got me a bit flustered, I lean in. "Prove it."

His face splits into a wide grin. "I'd love to, but my therapist wants me to take it easy." He takes another generous bite of the omelet. "Honestly, Kamila, this is really good. Maybe I was wrong about your cooking."

"You think?" I tease. "My abuela always said the way to a man's heart is through his stomach."

His eyes twinkle. "You trying to win my heart with this omelet then?"

Matching his playful tone, I counter, "Let's be real here, I won you over yesterday, and I didn't even have to feed you." I meet his eyes with a mischievous grin. "I guess all that's really needed is to dust off some cobwebs."

Our laughter fills the room.

"You know I was just teasing when I wrote that," Jackson admits. "You make it fun to get under your skin."

I roll my eyes. "I bet you've always been an ass to the women around you."

"I actually had a sparkling record of being sweet until you moved in here," he retorts.

I scoff. "Sure, you did." Sarcasm laces my tone.

"I'm serious," he insists. "In fact, I remember trying to impress this girl in high school. Sneaked out at midnight just to leave flowers on her porch."

I lean forward, intrigued. "Oh? And how did that go?"

He winces. "Let's just say I picked the wrong house. Ended up confessing my undying affection to a very shocked old lady."

I laugh, "You always were terrible with directions."

"Hey! It's not my fault all houses look the same in the dark."

I shake my head, still giggling. "Okay, how about this for a confession? Once, Luis and I decided to start a guacamole stand in our neighborhood."

Jackson raises an eyebrow. "A guacamole stand? Not lemonade?"

I nod, "Yep. We believed our guacamole recipe was revolutionary. Plus, we lived in a predominantly Latino neighborhood before moving to the city.

But here's the kicker: I accidentally added way too much lime in our first batch. People's faces!" I mimic a horrified expression. "But I blamed it all on Luis. He was pissed, but everyone believed the cute little girl with pigtails."

Jackson chuckles. "I bet Luis never lived that one down."

"Never," I confirm, giggling. "But speaking of embarrassing stories, tell me, Mr. Quarterback, about your early football days. I know there must be some juicy stories there."

He groans, rubbing the back of his neck. "Alright, but you can't laugh too hard. The first time I ever threw a football, I aimed for the tire swing. Instead, it went straight through the neighbor's window. They weren't thrilled."

I try and fail to stifle my laughter. "Oh, Jackson! No wonder you got into so much trouble. You were out in these streets breaking both elderly hearts and windows?"

He chuckles, his cheeks turning a shade redder. "Guilty on both counts. But hey, at least I'm consistent."

The mention of Luis earlier makes me reflect, "You know, growing up with Luis was a trip. We'd compete over everything since they moved next door in seventh grade - from grades to games. But the bond? It's unbreakable."

Jackson's eyes soften at this, perhaps recalling his own bonds, or maybe it's the realization of the one forming between us. Whatever it is, it's a comforting sight.

After breakfast, we lounge around the living room, watching a few of Jackson's old plays as he walks me through what was meant to happen in both the offense and defense runs.

"If you weren't playing football, what would you be doing," I ask, curiosity getting the better of me.

Jackson tilts his head in thought. "That's a good question. I was pretty good at painting all through high school and college. So maybe I'd be a struggling artist. Maybe even open my own gallery one day.

"Wow," I say. "I would've never guessed."

"What because I'm a jock I can't be into art?"

"I never once said that," I protest.

Jackson laughs. "No, but you thought it."

I look up at him smiling. "So now you read minds, huh?"

"I wish," he says, switching the TV off and sliding in closer to me. "Can I ask you a personal question?"

"Uh oh." I draw in an exaggerated breath. "What do you wanna know?"

Jackson shifts on the couch so he can face me. "Why haven't you been with anyone since you moved in here?"

I freeze. "What makes you think I haven't been with anyone?"

I haven't but it's just because I've been so busy, and I know from experience that when you work as many hours as I do, men tend to find other females to keep them entertained.

His gaze drops for a beat before returning to me. "Have you?"

I roll my eyes. "Not everyone needs to be as 'active' as you are to enjoy life," I snap.

His eyes fall again. "I wasn't trying to offend you," he clarifies. "I know it's cheesy, but I just find it hard to understand why someone hasn't already snatched you off the market." His eyes snap back to study my face with what looks to be panic in his eyes. "Unless you're not on the market. Fuck. Tell me you didn't let me sleep with you knowing you were –"

"I'm not with anyone," I clarify, cutting him off.

He releases a breath, and I sigh.

"I had a pretty serious relationship a few years ago that ended badly," I admit. "It left me feeling...vulnerable like I wasn't good enough for a man to care about me enough to allow me to pursue my dream and still be faithful."

Jackson's hand brushes against my thigh and a shiver travels up my spine. His eyes lock onto mine and the world fades.

"Anyone that ever made you feel like you didn't deserve the world was a fucking idiot."

I hold his gaze, nothing much had changed yet it felt like I was seeing him for the first time. And I like what I see.

Maybe even a little too much.

CHAPTER 11

"*I* need to show you something," Jackson says, looking away and breaking the magnetic effect.

"I swallow. "Okay."

His entire demeanor changes as he stands and leads me over to his room.

"Is this some weird way of luring me to your bed?" I tease.

Jackson chuckles, but it's not as full as he'd been laughing before. "Though I'd love to spread you over my bed and have you for both lunch and dinner, I need to come clean about something first." His Adam's apple bobs. "I at least owe you that much."

Confused, I nod and follow him over to his closet. He sets me to sit on his bed and then retrieves a box of something I couldn't make out.

"Before I show you this, remember I'm already injured," he says, a hint of a smile playing on his lips.

My eyebrow raises. "What's in the box, Jackson?"

He hands it to me, and my brows crease further as I pull out six different Victoria's Secret shopping bags with scandalous lingerie.

What the –

I don't know what I was expecting, but this wasn't it.

"Wait, what is this?" I ask, still not understanding what he's trying to tell me.

Jackson releases a breath. "I've been the one planting the underwear you've been finding around the apartment since you've been living here." He looks everywhere but at me. "Even the Espresso machine."

Finding this out last week would've pissed me off entirely and left me storming out to get some space. But, strange enough, right now I sorta just feel sorry for him.

How much of an ego boost had he needed that he had to go out of his way to do all that?

I groan. "You are sick, you know that? Why would you even do something like that?"

"I don't know," he admits with a shrug. "It started out as me trying to keep you at a distance then morphed into me enjoying getting you riled up."

He sighs. "Unfortunately, there's more."

Running his hand through his hair, he grabs the TV remote and powers it on.

The sounds that fill the room take me through a whole range of emotions in under a second. Recognition hits me the instant the woman screams Jackson's name. The TV screen is pitch black but the distinctly familiar track of moaning and what sounds to be a headboard pounding against a wall echoes through the room. The bass of his surround sound system shakes the walls in turn with the headboard bashing.

Jackson switches the TV off and I sit in silence, unsure of how to react. The underwear was one thing, but this is borderline mental.

"I can explain," Jackson says, realizing I had no obvious reaction.

I bite the inside of my bottom lip, before turning to him with raised eyebrows, still unsure what to think or say. Who have I been living with for the past eleven months?

Jackson drops on the bed next to me and I put a bit of space between us before I even realize what I'm doing.

His eyes slide shut, and he sighs.

"The day before you moved in here, I made a promise to Luis that I would do everything in my power to stay away from your bed and heart."

My jaw falls open. "Excuse me?"

"In my defense, when I agreed to his terms, I hadn't seen you in about ten years. I had been envisioning the same naïve seventeen-year-old girl that hated my guts for not seeing her how she saw me." He meets my eyes. "What I wasn't expecting was to see a grown, sophisticated, and sexy as all-get-out woman walk into my apparent fourteen fucking hours after agreeing to stay away from you. But Luis's friendship means the world to me, so I vowed to do whatever I had to do to keep my promise."

I sigh, slowly processing all Jackson's telling me, and working through all I feel about it all. I'd been obsessed with Jackson when I was in high school. He'd been my first crush. He'd been captain of the football at school then at home when he came over to hang out with Luis, he'd always been so nice to me. So, I took that to mean that he liked me too. His kindness continued even after he graduated, and I waited.

On the night before my senior prom, I had Natasha help me to create this spectacular display in the park across from his college dorm asking Jackson to be my date. But before he even got to see the sign we'd worked for hours preparing, I saw him and a busty blonde making out by a statue in the schoolyard. I'd been heartbroken. A week after that when Luis found out about it, he ripped me a new one and told me it wouldn't matter anyway as Jackson had gone off to play with the pros. He'd been drafted and moved to Chicago.

"Why even tell me any of this?" I ask, still figuring out my thoughts.

Jacksons shrugs. "I guess I just didn't want to lie to you anymore. And I'm sorry I ever even started this stupid setup."

He turns to face me and reaches for my hands. I don't pull away.

"I also need you to know the full truth before making the decision whether or not to allow me the privilege of sleeping with you again." The sincerity in his tone makes me smile.

"Nothing you've told me changes anything on my end," I confirm. "I am still a bit taken aback that you and Luis thought either of you had the authority to determine who I choose to allow in my bed." I meet his eyes. "But I am happy you told me the truth though."

A mischievous idea fills my head. "You are going to have to make it up to me somehow though."

Jackson studies me. "Oh?"

I nod. "And I know just the thing that would scream I'm sorry." I move to stand. "See I have under it under good authority that you should be resting and getting your protein in so that you're strong enough to return to the green next week."

A smile spreads across his lips when he realizes the direction, I'm taking this in.

"Lucky for you," I continue. "I just love feeding the needy." I bite back my laughter. "How about we play a little game of 'Simon Says' with Kamilla stakes."

Jackson's eyes follow me as I peel off my booty shorts to reveal a similar pair of black lacy panties to the ones he'd left on my Espresso Machine, but he doesn't say a word.

"The rules are simple," I continue. "Whatever Simon says you must do. And seeing this is payback for all the shit you've put me through since being here, you better damn well make sure you do the tasks given to the best of your ability. Do you understand the rules of the game?"

Jackson nods.

"Simon says speak," I demand.

"Yes ma'am," Jackson responds, a tinge of humor in his voice.

"Good boy," I praise.

I pull off my shirt before dancing out of my bra and panties. "Simon says lay back on the bed and get comfortable."

Jackson complies.

I climb up on the bed and straddle Jackson's face. His eyes widen in anticipation as I spread my legs wider to give him full access to my most intimate area.

"Simon says don't move," I command.

Again, he complies, laying still beneath me. The heat from his body emanates to my center, and my heart quickens in excitement at the thought of what is about to happen next. I reach down between us and guide his head forward until his mouth is positioned directly below my pussy.

"Simon says suck my pussy until my juices fill your mouth."

Jackson's tongue follows my instructions as it flickers out to taste me before retreating back into his warm mouth. The sensation of his tongue against my clit sends a quiver through me and I moan in pleasure, pushing down harder on top of him as he begins licking with more intensity.

"Simon says just like that," I say, my words breathy.

His hands grip firmly around my waist as he continues lapping at me like a thirsty animal, making sure not to miss a single bit of my sweet pussy juice that cascades down onto his tongue with each thrust of his eager mouth. My entire body trembles with ecstasy as he expertly flicks and sucks on my clit, causing pressure to build up inside me until I can take no more.

"Jackson!" I scream, my breathing fast and ragged.

Every muscle in my body clenches with pleasure as the waves

of pleasure wash over me. My body trembles as I move from my knees to tip toes so I can travel to his waiting erection.

"Simon says don't move."

Jackson watches from beneath me as I carefully climb around his shoulder before moving down to his waist and removing his shorts and boxers.

I lock my eyes on him as I position his dick at my entrance and slide my hips up and down on his shaft. I moan as I widen my legs allowing him to fill me up completely, stretching my tight walls to their limits.

Jackson groans.

"Simon says be quiet."

Jackson sucks his bottom lip into his mouth before biting down on his bottom lip. What I wouldn't give to taste those sweet lips of his again. But his last kiss wrecked me, and I wanted to take this experience all in.

His hands grip tightly around my waist as he thrusts into me with fierce intensity. The bed creaks beneath us as our rhythm quickens and the heat between us builds to an inferno-like level of passion.

"Simon didn't say to move," I protest between moans and gasps.

Jackson stills with a groan.

"Fuck Simon," he growls, flipping us over so that he is now on top while still inside of me.

Jackson picks up our pace, thrusting harder than before as he slams himself deep within me. Again, and again. Each thrust going deeper and harder than before. Building in pressure. The sound of our skin slapping drives me further and further up the wall until I explode. My body convulses and an uncontrollable giggle escapes my lips.

"Fuck. This pussy is going to be the fucking death of me," Jackson groans between thrusts.

He pounds into me with a final deep thrust that makes me scream.

"Fuck," he groins, his abs convulsing as his dick pulses his juices into me.

He crashes over next to me. Our bodies lay tangled together on sweat-soaked sheets for what feels like an eternity before either of us move or speak again. I have no clue where Jackson's head is at after all this, but I know I'm utterly fucked as somewhere within the split-second decision to do play Simon says and coming to terms with all that today was, my emotions entered the picture. Which sucks as Jacksom made it very clear that all he was interested in was a casual fuck. So, hoping to salvage whatever little is left of the fence around my heart. I jump to my feet and grab my clothes from the floor.

"You should get some rest," I say, heading for the door. Let's squeeze in a morning therapy sesh tomorrow before I leave. Say five o'clock."

Jackson opens his mouth as if to say something, but no sound comes out. Instead, he nods, and I take that as my cue to go figure out the shit show that's currently on repeat in my brain.

CHAPTER 12

I step out in the living room the next morning excited to see Kamilla again. Yesterday turned out to be the perfect day, and I was in a much lighter spirit with all the lies off my chest. There'd been a nagging need to ask Kamilla to spend the night in my bed, but I knew from all the conflicting emotions that had been swimming in my head that wouldn't have ended well for me. Especially seeing we agreed to no emotions, and no commitments. I'd much rather have her in my life and bed casually than not at all.

Kamilla stands next to the living room table, her dark brown hair pulled back into a neat ponytail, and her expression focused.

"Hey, you, how about we try something different today," she suggests, her gaze flicking between me and the assortment of therapy balls on the table. "I think we need to spice things up a bit."

"Spice things up?" I raise an eyebrow, curious about what she has in mind.

"Yeah, I want to evaluate your progress and see how strong your joints are outside of the adrenaline of our extra curricular activities." Kamilla says, a mischievous glint in her eyes.

"Okay," I say, with a wide smile. "What did you have in mind."

"How about a little competition?" I ask. "We'll each balance on one foot while holding six therapy balls. The goal is to see who drops fewer balls during the session. First to drop all their balls or drop their foot loses. We can do best of two. Think you can handle that?"

"Is that a challenge, Ms. Morallez?" I ask, teasing.

"Absolutely," she replies, smirking.

"Then you're on," I say, determined not to let her outdo me. "But how about we sweeten the deal?"

She raises an eyebrow, and I grin. "How about whoever loses has to buy the other one dinner."

I thought about biting the bullet and asking her on a real date the whole night. But this is perfect. It was going to be a blow to my ego but I'm throwing this competition.

I flash my eyebrows at Kamilla, and she smirks. "Seems like you're in the mood to spend some money, Mr. Taylor. You're on."

Kamilla splits the twelve balls between us, and we both take our positions, balancing on one foot as we hold the balls between our hands. She counts down from three, and we begin the exercise.

Immediately, it's clear that losing this competition won't be hard. As soon as I lift my leg, a weight presses on my groin. But I grit my teeth, refusing to let the pain get the better of me. Meanwhile, Kamilla seems to have no trouble at all, her lithe body steady and controlled.

"Come on, Jackson, you can do better than that," she teases playfully, her eyes twinkling with amusement. "I thought you were an athlete."

"Very funny," I grumble, concentrating on steadying my balance. "Just you wait - I'll catch up to you in no time."

"Is that right?" Kamilla chuckles, clearly enjoying the friendly competition. "Well then, may the best therapist win."

As we continue the exercise, dropping balls and laughing at each other's expense, I grow more and more enamored with this strong-willed, independent woman who has unexpectedly entered my life. There's something about her resilience that draws me in, making me want to be closer to her and help her to achieve her dreams.

At this point, Kamilla has four balls, and I have three. Though my intention is to lose, I still plan to give her a run for her money.

"Wow, Jackson, you're really showing off your skills here," Kamilla smirks, raising an eyebrow as I fumble with another ball.

"Hey, it's harder than it looks!" I retort, grinning despite my frustration. "Besides, you've dropped a few yourself."

"True, but I'm still ahead." She winks, and I smile at her feisty spirit. It's contagious, and I'm enjoying every moment of this friendly rivalry.

"So, what kind of movies do you like?" I ask, wanting to learn even more about her.

"Trying to distract me, are we?" She laughs.

My smile widens. "Hey, I'll take whatever advantage I can get."

"Anything but horror," she admits. "I'm more of a comedy, romance or action film person. What about you?"

"Same here," I reply, nodding in agreement. "All except for the romance. I enjoy a good laugh or an adrenaline rush. Speaking of which, have you seen the latest Marvel movie?"

"Of course! It was amazing!" Kamilla exclaims, her eyes lighting up with excitement.

"Why don't you like romance movies," she asks, wobbling slightly and dropping another ball.

I laugh. We're now down to three - two.

"I don't know. I feel romance flicks are for people who've found that special someone you know. When people like me watch them, who are already lonely, they either give you false hope or just leave you depressed."

Kamilla fumbles again but before her foot to touch the ground, I exaggerate a flinch and drop both my balls.

"Dang it," I yell, fighting the urge to smile. "I guess you won that one, but you said best of two, right?"

Kamilla smiles. "Yep. You actually did pretty good in that one. I'm impressed. Let's go ahead and switch sides."

"Ok doc," I tease, grabbing all our balls and sipping some water. "Ready to lose."

Kamilla's laughter fills the room, and the sound warms me from the inside out. I love making her laugh and smile.

"Just get in position," she retorts. "And start thinking about what you're getting me for breakfast.

Laughing I lift my opposite leg, this time the weight on my groin wasn't as bad as before.

"What's your go-to pizza topping?" Kamilla asks as soon as I steady myself.

"Now who's trying to distract who?" I tease, laughing. "Pepperoni and jalapeños. I like my pizza like I like my women — spicy with a bit of meat," I admit with a grin. "How about you?"

"Classic margherita," she replies. "Sometimes simple is best."

"Fair enough," I concede, chuckling. "You can't go wrong with a classic."

I wobble a bit and lose two balls.

"Come on, Jackson. You can do better than that," Kamilla cackles, making me laugh and lose another ball.

Down three ball, I struggle to regain my balance.

"You're distracting me on purpose," I protest, allowing yet another ball to fall.

My top ball wobbles and I shift to catch it but lose my balance and tumble to the ground, balls and all.

I roll over to my back, wallowing in my defeat and Kamilla's laughter bubbles up once more.

"Alright," she says, forcing down her laughter. "Let's wrap up our session with some stretches. Then we can continue our conversation over breakfast at the bistro down the street if you're up for it."

A huge smile stretches across my face. "Sounds like a good plan." I agree, excitement coursing through me at the prospect of spending more time with her outside the house.

"You better be," she says, with a laugh. "Cause based on your bet. Breakfast is on you."

Kamilla walks me through a stretch, and I mirror her movements, smiling.

"It was my bet and you won, fair and square. So, whatever you want it's on me."

"I think I like the sound of that," Kamilla teases, and I laugh.

"Try this stretch," she instructs, demonstrating the movement by extending one of her toned legs behind her while keeping the other bent beneath her. She leans forward, placing her hands on the mat for support. Her dark brown eyes never leave mine as she holds the pose.

Again, I mimic her movement, feeling the pull of my muscles. My gaze remains locked on hers, and the magnetic pull between us returns.

"Feels good, doesn't it?" Kamilla murmurs, a teasing smile playing on her lips.

"Definitely," I reply, trying to keep my voice steady as the intensity of our connection threatens to overwhelm me.

"Alright, let's face each other," Kamilla suggests, adjusting her position so that we're now sitting across from one another, our knees touching. "We'll do a partner stretch. Hold onto my hands, and we'll lean back and forth together."

"Sounds good," I say, reaching out to take her hands in mine. Her skin is warm and soft, and the touch sends a jolt of desire through me. As we begin to synchronize our movements, our breathing falls into rhythm, and the space between us closes, inch by inch.

"We should get going," Kamilla says, breaking the spell.

A pang of disappointment hits me as I wanted to feel her lips on mine. But I remind myself she's only in this for a casual fling.

I force a smile. "Sure, lets go."

The bistro is a quaint little spot, its brick walls lined with old photos and painted signs from times gone by. The familiar chime of the doorbell announces our arrival, and the waitress, an older woman with a smile that seems permanently etched onto her face, waves at us from behind the counter.

"Morning, Mrs. Bennett," Kamilla says with a warm smile.

"Morning, dear. And Jackson! I haven't seen you in ages," Mrs. Bennett exclaims, her eyes twinkling.

I laugh, "I got injured a few weeks ago. Been busy with my therapy sessions with the city's finest," pointing to Kamilla.

Mrs. Bennett nods, "Ah, so you're the one helping this old sport get back on his feet. Good to know he's in good hands."

Kamilla and I share a glance. If only Mrs. Bennett knew how deep in her hands I really was. Or my cock, was to be precise.

"Well, he's definitely a handful," Kamilla quips.

I stifle a laugh, and Kamilla's eyes widen a tad before regaining her composure.

"But he's coming along nicely," Kamilla confirms.

Mrs. Bennett assigns us a waitress who leads us to a booth near the window. The morning sun streams in, lighting up the table. As we slide in, I look out and notice a park just across the street, a familiar spot from our childhood.

"Do you remember hanging out there during high school?" I ask, pointing.

Kamilla follows my gaze and chuckles, "Oh yeah, that park has seen its fair share of drama." Her face falls for a brief moment, before she bored a smile. I was about to figure out if I'd said something wrong when she began to speak.

Speaking of, did you ever notice a massive sign there around prom season?"

I furrow my brows, thinking back. "Not that I recall... why?"

She rolls her eyes, then sighs. "I might have, sort of, kind of, made a big sign asking you to prom my senior year."

My eyes widen. "You what? When was this?"

She smirks, "Yeah, the night before my prom. But I chickened out at the last minute. Saw you with some full chested blonde, and well, I figured you had plans."

I wrack my brain, and the memory of a fleeting kiss with someone from my literature class surfaces.

"Oh, that must have been Jess! We worked on quite a few projects together back then. She was my tutor," I clarify. "Wait, so you were going to ask me to your prom?"

She shrugs, "I had a huge crush on you in high school. I thought asking you to prom would be my big romantic gesture. But you were always with Luis when you were around. So, I hatched a plan to ask you while you were back at your dorm."

"Damn, if I'd known that, I would've—"

"Taken me as your kid sister?" she interrupts with a teasing grin.

Kamilla rolls her eyes, and I laugh.

"Okay, okay, you got me there," I admit. "But seriously, I wish I'd known. It would've been fun!"

A momentary silence ensues as our orders arrive – her classic Margherita and my Spicy Pepperoni.

"This city always brings back good memories," I say as the waitress leaves. "Remember when Luis tried to climb up the water tower because he wanted to see if he could spot his house from there?" I chuckle.

Kamilla groans, "Oh, don't remind me! Mom almost had a heart attack!"

'And remember when you tried to color his hair blue while he was asleep, but it ended up being green?" I counter.

She bursts out laughing. "He'd been an ass to me earlier that day and I told him he'd regret it. His face the next morning was priceless!"

We finish our pizza slices between fits of laughter and more shared memories. So much of our teenaged lives have been intertwined due to Luis yet our paths couldn't have been more different.

"Ready to get out of here," I ask, glancing at the time on my phone.

Kamilla's phone goes off before she can respond. Nodding he grabs her phone from her purse and scowls. She turns the screen to face me.

"It's your friend," she says, her tone bitter. "I don't think I'm ready to talk to him yet. Cause if I do, I'm gonna rip him a new one for trying to control my personal life through you."

I sigh. "Except you don't officially know about that, remember?"

She hits ignore and drops the phone back in her purse. "And that is why I'm not answering until I'm ready."

My phone goes off, and I glance around the bistro, already knowing who it is. Luis's name flashes across my caller ID. Luis never calls me looking for Kamilla so to be calling me right after her was worrying to say the least.

"Hey, Lu," I answer, hoping like fuck I sound casual. "Sup?"

"Big things man," he responds.

I put the phone on speaker then lower the volume.

"But I don't want to tell you over the phone," he continues.

Kamilla's eyebrows raise before locking eyes with mine.

"Okay, that must be some big news," I say. "How about I meet you at –"

"I was more thinking I could stop by the apartment later for dinner with you and Kam."

That gives me pause. As far as Luis knows, we never eat dinner together.

I release a nervous laugh. "Well if you can get your sister to agree, I'll be there."

"Perfect," see you then,' Luis singsongs into the phone before ending the call.

Kamilla and my eyes lock, concern etched over her face.

This is lining up to be an interesting day.

CHAPTER 13

KAMILLA

I pace my room after work, the weight of the growing feelings for Jackson in spite of my promise to keep things casual a heavy burden on my chest. My fingers drum against my thigh as I contemplate whether to keep this all to myself or share it with the Sisterhood.

"I gave Jackson my word to keep it a secret..." The words tumble out of my mouth as I continue to weigh the pros and cons in my head. My eyes wander to my phone resting on the bed, beckoning me to come clean to my girls.

"Ugh, what am I even thinking?" I mutter under my breath. But then again, its not like Latalia, Natasha, or Trina is gonna take anything I say back to Jackson or Luis. And their input has never steered me wrong before...

"Okay, I'm doing it," I say, grabbing my phone and opening the Sisterhood chat.

Me:
Hey, ladies, I need your advice on something.

WITHIN SECONDS, three sets of typing bubbles appear, and I swallow. No turning back now.

LATALIA:
What's up, Kam? You know we've got your back.

TRINA:
Spill the tea, girl!

NATASHA:
Go ahead, babe. We're here for you.

I TAKE A DEEP BREATH, reminding myself that these women are my rocks. They've helped me grow into the person I am today, and their love and loyalty have never wavered. Even if they're painfully honest about how stupid this whole set up is. I close my hand around the phone to still my trembling fingers.

Me:
Okay, so here's the thing... Jackson and I have sorta made a secret agreement.

A MINUTE GOES by without a response, but it feels like twenty.

LATALIA:

Wait, what? You and Jackson? The same guy you've been avoiding for weeks?

Me:
Yep, that's the one. We agreed to... well, it's kind of a private arrangement to benefit both of us.

TRINA:

Kamila Gabrella Morallez! Spill the details right now before I explode.

Me:
Alright, alright... We agreed to engage in a no-strings-attached, purely physical casual sex.

AGAIN, the chat goes silent, and for a moment, I worry I've crossed some unspoken line that even the Sisterhood can't decipher. But then the floodgates burst open.

NATASHA:

Kamila Morallez! I didn't think you had it in you!

. . .

LATALIA:

Girl, I am shocked and impressed lol

TRINA:

Who would've thought. Our very own Kamila, stepping out of her comfort zone like this?

Me:
So y'all don't think I've lost all my nuts?

LATALIA:

Sounds like you've gain a pair of nuts rather than losing them lol. On a more serious note, though, how does the agreement make you feel? Do you feel like you're doing something wrong or is it something you really want?

Me:
Oh, I wanted this.

LATALIA:

Wanted?

Me:
Sigh. I don't know guys. At first it was all fun and games but...

NATASHA:

Oh honey, are you getting real feelings for him?

TRINA:

You need to be careful, babe. These types of arrangements can get messy fast.

Me:

It's not like that. Sigh. At least I don't think so. We're just having fun together. Maybe a little too much, but there was a stupid promise Luis had him make to stay away from me which is why he's been going out of his way to be such an ass. And, to be honest, though I was initially pissed at both of them. Since Jackson's come clean, he's been ... I don't know... different somehow. Sigh. It's all gotten so complicated. and I feel really guilty for keeping it from you guys for as long as I have.

LATALIA:

Luis has always been a piece of work. No surprise there. I'm more concerned about you. But what you're saying is you decided to tell us all this now after you've been giving up that good good despite all that because you 'don't' think you have feelings for Jackson? Okay. I'll let you tell yourself whatever you need to believe, but I'm not buying it for a second.

LATALIA'S SARCASM screams at me even through her text, and I smile.

NATASHA:

Well, Kam, if you're going to do this, you might as well enjoy it. Those muscles of his are no joke.

TRINA:

Right lol. I mean, you could probably use Jackson as a human jungle gym if you wanted to.

Me:

Oh my god, lol. Y'all better stop with all that. He's still Jackson. This changes nothing but our private interactions.

NATASHA:

Hmm-mm. Fine.

But seriously, Kam, if you decide to go through with this, just remember to have fun. And for fuck's sake set a timer for your birth control.

LATALIA:

What Natasha said. We don't need any God babies until you both are ready to admit to yourselves that whatever is going on between you is something more. Once all that's covered, have fun with it. Its about time that man gives you something other than stress.

Me:

Ain't that the truth? But guys, what if I do catch feelings? Hell, what if he does?"

NATASHA:

Just be careful. As Trina said, these things can get complicated, and none of us want to see you get hurt.

I SIGH, running a hand through my dark curls.

Me:

I know. I just... I don't know what to do. Part of me wants to take the plunge and see if Jackson would even want to give a relationship a real go, but another part is terrified of getting my heart broken again. Especially seeing I was the one who pushed for this whole thing to be casual.

LATALIA:

Aww honey. I know that position well. But only you can make that decision. Whatever you choose, just remember that your happiness comes first. And we'll be here for you, no matter what.

Me:

Sigh. Thanks guys. I guess I'll see how the next few days go, Then I'll make up my mind.

TRINA:

Just promise me you won't let fear hold you back from even trying if it's something you really want to explore.

Me:

I promise.

· · ·

THERE WAS a knock on the front door that I figured was Luis as Jackson would have his key.

Me:
Gotta go ladies. We're hosting Luis for dinner and seeing he has no clue about our arrangement it's about to be one heck of a performance. Sigh.
Pray for me.

PLUGGING my phone in to charge, I give myself a final look over in my bedroom mirror before nodding and moving to greet my brother at the door. This is the first time I'm seeing or speaking to him since Jackson told me about his little forced promise. And though I'd love to rip him a new one, doing that would throw Jackson all the way under the bus. So, though we will be having a stern chat at some point in the future about his delusional hold on my personal life, tonight is not the night.

CHAPTER 14

JACKSON

The sound of laughter echoes through the apartment from the TV as I swing open the front door with our dinner in hand. Kamilla and I had agreed earlier to order dinner from Luis's favorite restaurant as he loved his food just about as much as Kamilla. The hope is that his favorite BBQ brisket will keep his attention away from the tension or lack there of between me and Kamilla. About an hour ago, I called Luis propositioning it to have it seem like his idea.

Luis's familiar grin widens upon seeing me, and he rushes to grab the bag from me before pulling me into a bear hug.

"Jackson, my man!" Luis exclaims, slapping my back. "It's been too long, bro."

"Too long indeed," I agree, sarcasm lacing my tone as I release him from our embrace. "A whole fucking week."

I force a laugh as I step past him and into the apartment, ignoring every instinct in me to properly greet Kamilla.

Kamilla rolls her eyes in my direction as soon as both Luis

and I were in full view. "Great, I take it this means you'll also be joining us for dinner?"

"Indeed, I am," I retort, forcing a smirk onto my face. "Wouldn't want to miss out on a lovely dinner with my two favorite people."

"Favorite? Please, you can barely stand to be in the same room as me," Kamilla scoffs, rolling her eyes.

"Right back at you," I shoot back, trying to ignore the way my heart clenches at our fake animosity.

"Alright, alright, you two," Luis interjects, buying into the fake tension between us. "Let's just enjoy the evening, okay?"

"Fine," Kamilla mutters, turning back to the fridge to grab three beers.

"Great," I say, still sporting my smirk. "Let's set the table, then."

As we set the table, I steal glances at Kamilla when she isn't looking. Our pretended hatred for each other is just that—a pretense. But for now, we keep up the act, unwilling to let whatever this was between us show in front of Luis.

"Okay, everything's ready," Kamilla announces, lifting the platter she'd transferred the takeout into and carrying it to the dining table. "Let's eat."

"Finally, I'm starving!" Luis exclaims, rubbing his hands together. He takes a seat at the table.

"Bon appétit," I say, the air growing thick with tension as we take our seats and begin to serve ourselves. Luckily, Luis dives into a story about the week of practice that I missed, clearly still unaware of the underlying emotions that I'm struggling to keep hidden.

"Jackson, man, you should have seen it," Luis says, chuckling. "I swear, it was like watching a ballet performance on the field!"

'Sounds like quite the spectacle," I reply, grinning at the mental image his words paint. But my gaze keeps drifting back towards Kamilla, drawn by her familiar magnetic pull. Her eyes flicker up to meet mine for just a heartbeat before she looks away, a quick smile crossing her lips.

"Kam, I swear you are glowing." Luis teases, twirling another forkful of spaghetti with a piece of brisket. "Is there a new man I need to watch out for in your life?"

Kamilla's eyes meet mine for a beat.

"There sure is," she admits with a smile.

I swallow hard, and Luis glances up in her direction."

"His name is learn to mind your own bloody business," she teases, a small smile playing on her lips. She glances at me again, but this time, our eyes lock for a moment longer. The unspoken message is clear—we both know we're playing a dangerous game, but neither of us can seem to resist.

A brief silence falls over the table as we return to eating. Each stolen glance, each casual brush of skin against skin as we pass dishes or reach for drinks, sends a jolt of electricity through my veins. I can feel Kamilla's gaze lingering on me when she thinks I'm not paying attention, and I revel in the knowledge that she clearly wants me just as much as I want her.

"Hey, Jackson, you alright?" Luis asks, snapping me out of my thoughts. "You've been pretty quiet."

"Uh, yeah, I'm fine," I respond, trying to regain my composure. "Just, uh, thinking about my doctor's check-in appointment tomorrow. Really want to be cleared to get back on the green, you know."

"Oh, I get it man, in fact, my position on the football field, or lack there of, is a big part of why I wanted us to have dinner together tonight," Luis says, grinning.

I raise an eyebrow. "What do you mean? Did something happen."

Kamilla shifts to study her brother. "Maybe you're the one with the glow. What did you do?"

Luis's smile widens. "I got an interesting call from my agent today."

"Okay," I say growing impatient. The last time Luis was this giddy I was moving back to New York to play with the Giants.

"The Cardinals has made me a very generous offer to play with them after my contract ends at the end of the season," Luis continues, beaming. "Like seven figure generous."

My gaze jumps to Kamilla. Her eyes fall to her plate. For as long as I've known Luis, he's always done everything in his power to stay in New York to be close to Kamilla, more so after their parents passed.

"That's great man," I say, genuinely happy for him.

Kamilla's eyes remain glued to her stalled fork. Everything in me screams for me to comfort her, but I fight the urge and try to focus on Luis.

"Thanks man," Luis says. "Nothing is set in stone yet, but it'd be dumb to not at least consider it.

"The Cardinals as in the team in Phoenix?" Kamilla asks, finally bringing her gaze to meet her brother once more. "As in halfway across the country?"

Luis leans back in his chair, studying Kamilla. His eyes search her face.

"Phoenix, Kam." Luis repeats, rubbing the back of his neck, a gesture that betrays his discomfort. "But it's just an opportunity, not a done deal. We've always talked about embracing opportunities, right?"

Kamilla's fingers play with the frayed edges of the tablecloth, her eyes lost in the woven threads. "Phoenix is halfway across the country, Luis," she says, her voice trembling a bit.

Inside, I'm torn. Part of me is thrilled at the prospect of Luis being further away. It would give Kamilla and I a chance to explore what's between us without constant oversight. But seeing her this shaken brings a sting of guilt to my core.

Luis scoots his chair closer to his sister. "Hey, hey," he murmurs, tucking a stray strand of her hair behind her ear. "It's just an offer. We have time. Months, even. And you know you could always take over my place if I do decide to go, right?"

She blinks at him, the threat of tears gleaming. "Your studio?"

"Yeah, the lease is good. And you've been wanting your own space for a while, haven't you?"

She sniffs, nodding. "Yeah, but not at the expense of you moving so far away."

All I can think about is how much I want to cradle her in my arms. To tell her that I'll be there for her, no matter what. But instead, my voice comes out detached, "Maybe this could be good for both of you. Change isn't always a bad thing."

Kamilla's gaze flicks to mine, a challenge in her eyes. It's as if she's daring me to admit there's more behind my words. But I hold her gaze, my mask firmly in place as Luis nods in my direction.

"Look, Kam," Luis starts, his voice softening, "I've watched over you since we were kids, especially after..." He trails off, not needing to mention the shared pain of their parents' passing. "But maybe this is the universe telling us it's time to chart our own paths. To see who we are when we're not leaning on each other so much."

She bites her lower lip. "I hate it when you get all philosophical on me."

He chuckles. "It's part of my charm."

The weight of the conversation bears down on me, and I push back my chair. "I think I'll head to the bathroom. Give you two some time to talk." It's only half a lie.

Inside the confines of the bathroom, the world blurs. The reflection staring back at me from the mirror is a man at war with himself. I splash cold water onto my face, hoping it might quell the tempest of emotions threatening to consume me.

"Get a grip, Jackson," I mutter.

My hands grip the edges of the sink, grounding me. I draw in a deep breath. Tonight, was never about declarations or coming out with the truth. It was about dinner. About being there for Kamilla, even if from a distance. But the thought of Luis leaving, paired with the guilt of all that I'm starting to feel for Kamilla is crushing.

"She's not ready," I remind myself. Kamilla hasn't given any indication she wants our arrangement to be more, to be public. And I won't push her, especially not tonight, not with everything else on her plate.

Steeling myself, I take one last glance in the mirror confirming my role. My facade must remain intact, at least for now.

I return to the dining area, finding Luis and Kamilla in a tight embrace. As I'm about to leave to give them space, Kamilla's eyes meet mine over Luis's shoulder with a flicker of gratitude.

I clear my throat. "You guys good?"

Kamilla nods, pulling away from her brother. "Yeah, we're good." She glances between Luis and me. "We always are."

She flashes me a sly smile, and I nod. Luis, still seemingly oblivious, drains the last of his beer and releases a satisfied sigh.

"Well, I should get going. Early practice tomorrow. Good luck on your doctor's visit man. Hopefully, we see you at practice after."

"Here's hoping," I say, my voice strained. My fingers itch for him to leave so I can comfort Kamilla. "Thanks for coming, man. We'll catch up tomorrow after I leave the clinic."

"Definitely," Luis agrees, clapping me on the shoulder. He turns to his sister. "We're really good, right?"

"Of course," she replies, her voice steady despite the storm raging in her eyes. "Don't worry about me. Get home safe."

"Alright, see you guys later," Luis says, stepping toward the door.

"Bye," Kamilla and I chorus.

Our eyes widens a hare before forcing smiles, praying like hell Luis didn't pick up on our eagerness to get rid of him.

CHAPTER 15

The door closes with a soft click behind Luis, and the vast expanse of the apartment shrinks around Jackson and me. The afterglow of the chandelier casts a muted, golden hue, accentuating the sharp angles of Jackson's face as he watches me.

Jackson's fingers drum on the table's edge, a rhythm too fast, too erratic. His gaze is heavy, contemplative, as if he's trying to decipher a complex puzzle.

"Phoenix, huh?" he begins, voice low, each word calculated.

I shrug, trying to play my feelings off as nonchalance, but the tremor in my hands betrays me as I fidget with the frayed edges of the tablecloth. "It's not so far, just a few states over." I force a laugh, brittle and fragile, hoping to sound convincing.

He stands, the chair grating against the wooden floor as he approaches me. His towering presence becomes an anchor, grounding me. Shadows dance across his face.

"It's more than just the distance, Kammie," he murmurs,

fingertips brushing my cheek, sending electric tingles down my spine.

I lean into his touch, craving the comfort only he can offer. "Everything's changing so fast, Jack. It's like the ground's shifting beneath me." I hesitate, then add, "Beneath us."

The faintest hint of a smile plays on his lips. "Change can be daunting, I know, but it's also inevitable. And sometimes, it's necessary."

I search his eyes, trying to decipher the thought swirling in his head. "Is that your way of saying this could be good for us?"

His fingers curl around my chin, tilting my face up to meet his gaze. "It's my way of saying whatever happens, we'll navigate it. Together."

His assurance sends warmth spreading through me, thawing the chill of uncertainty. "You always have a way with words," I tease, my voice soft.

He chuckles, the sound deep and comforting. "Only when I'm around you."

My heart flutters. But then a pang of unease pricks me, and I pull back. "You don't think Luis suspects anything, do you?"

Jackson sighs, running a hand through his tousled hair. "He's observant, but he's also preoccupied with his own life right now."

Silence stretches between us, filled only with the soft hum of the refrigerator and our synchronized breathing.

"I don't want to hide anymore, Jackson," I confess, biting my lip. The words hang in the air, charged and heavy. "I'm a grown woman, I should be able to openly sleep with whomever I please. If Luis is taking advantage of all his opportunities why can't I."

His eyes search mine. "Neither do I. But we'll decide when the time's right, together."

He pulls me close, wrapping me in his embrace. The familiar scent of his cologne fills my senses like a calming balm.

"Promise me," I mumble into his chest, "that whatever happens, this..." I gesture between us, "...won't change."

He tightens his grip, his breath warm against my ear. "I promise. Nothing and no one can come between us."

"I can't believe Luis might leave. He's always been there for me, especially after our parents..."

Jackson's fingers trace soothing circles on my back. "People evolve, Kammie. Maybe it's time for him to find his path, just as it's time for us to find ours."

I look up at him, tears threatening to spill. "But what if things go wrong? What if he gets hurt out there, all alone?"

He brushes away a stray tear, his touch gentle. "He's resilient, just like you. And he's got you cheering from the sidelines. That's more than enough motivation."

A soft chuckle escapes my lips. "Always the optimist, aren't you?"

He smirks, the playful glint back in his eyes. "Only when it comes to you two. I've seen you two conquer so much both together and apart."

"The same goes for you, you know," I begin, squeezing his hand. "I believe in you. I truly do. You're strong enough to make it back onto the field, and your dedication to your recovery is clear. I have no doubt the doctor won't agree when you check in tomorrow."

A small smile forms on his lips, and he leans closer, pressing a soft kiss to my cheek.

"Thank you," he whispers, his breath warm against my skin. "Your support means everything to me."

We share a tender gaze, gratitude radiating from him and filling my chest with warmth. His hands run down my arms then cups the small of my back to pull me into him.

"I'd love to show you just how much your support means to me," he growls before lowering his lips onto mine.

The taste of him fills my senses – the tang of sweat mingling with the musk of his cologne. Our tongues tangle together, exploring each other's mouths with fervor and hunger. His strong arms wrap around me, pressing my body against his as my fingers tangle in his hair, pulling him closer.

The heat of his arousal presses against my thigh. Desire courses through me like wildfire. His hands roam my body, leaving a trail of goosebumps in their wake as they slip under my shirt to caress the sensitive skin of my back.

As our kiss deepens, it's clear that we're both teetering on the edge of surrender, willing to throw caution to the wind for a taste of something more profound, something real.

"Kamilla," Jackson whispers against my lips, his voice barely audible as he pulls back just enough to look into my eyes. "I want you – all of you."

His words send shivers down my spine, the vulnerability in his gaze making my heart race. Something about this, the intensity, the vulnerability, it all feels different somehow. My fingers tremble as I reach for the hem of his shirt, pulling it up and over his head. His chest is a masterpiece of sculpted muscle, each ridge and valley calling out for my touch. I trace my fingertips along the planes of his abs, and he quivers beneath my touch.

"Jackson," I murmur, leaning in to press my lips to his once more. "I want you too."

The urgency between us grows, our breaths coming in short gasps as he fumbles with my belt, zipper and pants button. My clothes are discarded, the sound of fabric hitting the floor punctuating the air around us. In a matter of moments, I'm naked and vulnerable, my body trembling with need.

"I don't want to fuck you tonight," he admits, holding my gaze. "Let me make love to you." He lowers his lips to my forehead in a gentle kiss. "Feel every sensation." His kiss moves lower, this time behind my ear before nibbling on my earlobe.

"Please," I whisper, unable to form any coherent thoughts beyond the overwhelming desire to be with him completely.

He descends my body with tender kisses, etching a path from my neck to my chest. His mouth laps at my nipple with gentle suction, and I soften beneath him before pulling back to take me in.

Smiling, he peels his pants off allowing his dick jolts out thick, stiff and at attention. His gaze holds mine as he takes my hand in his, guiding it to stroke the length of his dick.

My fingers trace down Jackson's length as I lower myself to my knees, eliciting a groan from deep in his throat. His breath catches as I take him fully into my mouth. I move with increased fervor, my lips and tongue dancing around his dick. He grips my hair between his fingers and his hips flex in time with my movements.

His shaft thickens between my lips and his dick thrums beneath me. He pulls at my head as his growl vibrates through my core.

"When I cum it will be inside your clenching pussy," he says, his tone breathy and deep.

My heart leaps into my throat as he swoops me up and drops me onto the edge of the dining table. I don't have time to process his scorching gaze before he sinks to his knees between my thighs, sending a jolt of awareness through me.

His tongue licks circles around my clit, dragging moans from deep in my soul. He teases me, tormenting me with feather-light licks that leave me on the brink of climax but never pushing far enough for release.

While still teasing my clit, he slides two fingers inside of me, igniting an inferno within. My hips grind down against him, desperate for more. I grip the edges of the table, my insides clenching as my orgasm threatens.

"Oh God, Jackson," I moan. "That feels so fucking good."

His tongue continues it's torment, pushing me to the brink of no return. I ravage his name in a plea for mercy, my core throbbing with an intensity I can't contain. He eats me like he knows no other way, pushing through my pain and pleas until finally I shatter beneath his lips. His breath is hot against my inner thigh as he plants light kisses along my leg until my tremors subside.

Jackson takes my hand and leads me to my bedroom, our gazes never straying from one another's as we lower ourselves onto the soft sheets. He positions himself above me, his strong arms supporting his weight as he leans down to claim my lips once more. Our bodies fit together like pieces of a puzzle, every curve and angle aligning in a way that feels as if we were always meant to be this close.

"Are you ready?" he asks, his eyes searching mine for any hint of hesitation.

"More than I've ever been," I reply, the certainty in my voice surprising even myself.

Our lips meld together in a tender embrace. His tongue darts between my parted lips, tasting every inch of my mouth as he drinks me in. My body hums with pleasure as I arch against him, my juices still sweet on his lips.

He breaks the kiss to trail his lips along my neck, nipping at my skin and sending tingles down my spine. His hand grazes up my side before gripping onto one of my breasts, teasing it with gentle caresses that sets fire to every nerve-ending in its wake. His other hand moves leisurely down my stomach, dipping below my waist to tease me once more.

Finally, Jackson positions himself above me, his strong arms supporting his weight as he leans down to claim my lips once more. Our bodies collide together in a heated battle for control and dominance that only serves to heighten our arousal further.

He slides inside of me with a primitive growl, filling me with a slow, deliberate motion. Jackson guides our bodies together, each inch of him filling me with indescribable pleasure. His hips slowly roll against mine, his thick erection parting my slick folds.

He lowers his lips to mine mid-stroke, and I moan into his mouth. My fingers dig into the firm muscles of his back as he begins to thrust harder in and out of me, each movement bringing a new wave of pleasure coursing through my body.

"God, Kamilla," Jackson groans, his voice strained with lust. "You're so tight, so perfect."

Heat floods my cheeks, but any embarrassment is quickly drowned by the sensations he elicits within me. As the pace of his thrusts quickens, I lose myself in the primal rhythm of our bodies colliding.

"Jackson," I pant, struggling to form coherent thoughts amidst the haze of pleasure. "Don't stop, please."

"Never," he promises, his strong hands gripping my hips, guiding our movements with a sense of urgency. "I need you too, baby. Let me drive you over the edge."

Our eyes lock as I nod, granting him permission to take control. Jackson adjusts his position, pressing one of my legs up towards my chest, opening me even further to his deep, powerful thrusts. The change in angle sends jolts of ecstasy through my core.

"Right there," I gasp, my nails raking down the length of his biceps. "Please, don't stop."

"Anything for you," he growls in response, his own breath coming in ragged pants.

Jackson's strokes become more forceful, driving into me with a passion that leaves me reeling, teetering on the edge of release. His thumb finds my swollen clit, rubbing it in tight circles as he continues to pound into me.

"Jackson, I'm so close," I whimper, my body tensing.

"Let go, baby," he urges, his eyes dark with desire. "Cum for me."

His words are all it takes to send me tumbling over the edge, my orgasm crashing through me like a tidal wave. My inner muscles clench around Jackson's dick, drawing a deep moan from him as he follows suit, spilling his hot seed inside me.

As our bodies begin to still, we cling to one another, our

chests heaving. I rest my head on Jackson's shoulder. My heart is still pounding in my chest as Jackson pulls away from our passionate embrace. His eyes, which moments ago were filled with tenderness and desire, now hold a strange mix of what seems like panic or fear… regret, maybe?

"Thank you, for letting me in," he says, his voice strained. "I… I need to get some rest before my doctor's visit in the morning."

"Jackson?" I ask, confusion clouding my thoughts. "Is everything okay?"

He hesitates, clearly struggling with something internally. "Yeah, yeah, it's just… there's a lot on my mind right now."

"Can we talk about it?" My concern grows as I reach out to touch his arm, but he steps back, avoiding my touch.

"Later," he promises, his eyes avoiding mine as he retreats to his room, closing my bedroom door behind him.

CHAPTER 16

KAMILLA

I've been in my head all night. Jackson took me over the emotional edge last night after asking me to trust him. And I loved every minute of it. That is until he jumped back over the line in his mind after we made love. I got up earlier than normal hoping to talk it through with him before he left but by the time I got to his bedroom he was already gone, leaving my mind in an utter state of confusion.

The sun casts golden streaks across the sky as I unlock the door to my clinic. My lips still tingle from Jackson's kiss last night, and I smile as I remember the feeling of his strong arms wrapped around me. But as I step inside and switch on the lights, a nagging sense of unease begins to settle in my chest. I glance at my watch before checking my roster. There is about fifteen minutes before my first client. I sigh. I had hoped to get here with very little time left so I could occupy my mind with things other than Jackson.

I glance at my phone. By now his doctor's appointment

should be over, but he's still not called or texted. I know I should give him space to process. But I just wish he'd text to at least let me know he's okay. If even just as his physiotherapist.

Taking a deep breath, I decide to be proactive and dial Jackson's number. My heart races as the phone rings, hoping this call might clear up some of the confusion surrounding us.

"Hey Kam," a familiar voice answers, but it isn't Jackson's.

"Hey, Luis," I say, recognizing my brother's voice. "Is Jackson there?"

A fit of female giggling with what sounds to be Jackson's voice bursts out in the background.

"Hmm," he replies, drawing out the syllable. "Jackson's a bit… preoccupied at the moment, but I can tell you that his doctor's appointment went well. He's been cleared, so no worries there."

"Oh, that's great news," I respond, hoping my confliction isn't evident in my tone. "I'm glad he's okay." I'd been hoping to talk to Jackson to at least gauge his reactions.

Giggling sounds out again, and a pang of embarrassment passes through me. Is that why he hasn't had time to call me? I'm so stupid to think that Jackson could be serious about me. Especially when he pushed so hard for our arrangement to be a secret.

"Anything else you need?" Luis asks, dragging me back to the present.

"Um, no," I stutter, embarrassment settling in my stomach. "That was all. Thanks again."

"By the way," Luis says, shifting gears, "Jackson mentioned that he's going out tonight. You know, to celebrate his good news with some friends. So, you may have the apartment to yourself for once. I'll try to keep him out for as long as he lets me."

"Friends?" I ask, trying not to sound too interested.

"Uh, yeah," he hesitates, as if sensing my concern. "I think there might be a few of the boys who want to welcome back their quarterback and a few cheerleaders too."

There it is – the sting of jealousy, raw and unexpected. My

chest tightens at the thought of Jackson partying with other women, all while avoiding me after our passionate night together. I force a laugh, attempting to mask my emotions. "Oh, that's sweet. I could use a peaceful night at home. "

"Definitely," Luis agrees. "Anyway, I gotta go, sis. Take care, okay?"

"Sure, you too," I reply, my voice wavering a tad. I end the call and toss my phone onto the desk, trying to ignore the sinking feeling in my stomach.

I pace around my clinic, as my thoughts race between the lingering warmth of Jackson's kiss and the cold reality of his avoidance. Why would he share such an intimate moment with me, only to distance himself afterward? The unanswered questions gnaw at me, leaving me on edge.

Taking a deep breath, I attempt to regain control over my racing heart. It doesn't matter what Jackson does or who he spends time with. What we had was just a casual fling. A fling that I agreed to.

"Focus, Kamilla," I whisper, clenching my fists at my sides. "Don't let him get to you."

Yet, despite my best efforts, I can't shake the image of Jackson laughing and flirting with other women. And as much as I want to deny it, I care about what happens between us. The truth is, I want him; not just for a fleeting night of passion, but for something more. And the thought of losing him to someone else is too painful to bear.

"Damn it," I mutter. "Why does this have to be so complicated?"

Jackson is a grown man. He can go out and control himself. This could be the perfect situation to know for sure if anything that I've been feeling between us has been real or not. If I want to really give this a go with Jackson, I'll have to learn to trust that he won't do anything to hurt me. For my own sanity, I have to believe that's true.

Pulling in a breath, I straighten and prepare for my next client, promising myself that no matter what happens with Jackson, I'll continue to strive for success and happiness – on my own terms.

CHAPTER 17

I stifle a groan as the bass from the music vibrates through my chest to every nerve of my body. Flashing lights dance across my apartment, casting a chaotic kaleidoscope of colors on the walls. Luis and I are surrounded by cheerleaders, all laughing, dancing, and enjoying themselves. All I can think of is Kamilla and going home. Last night was amazing until it wasn't, mainly because I was hit by a fucking hint of an emotion, I thought I'd buried a long time ago.

"Hey, Jackson!" Chelsea shouts over the pounding beat, grabbing my arm. "Come dance with us!"

I force a smile and join in, trying to show enthusiasm as I move to the rhythm. But my thoughts remain on Kamilla, her soft lips pressed against mine, the way her hands felt tangled in my hair.

"Jackson!" another cheerleader calls out. "You're so quiet! What's up?"

"Nothing," I lie, attempting to engage in small talk. "Just taking it all in."

"You sure?" she asks, her eyes narrowing. "You seem a little...distracted." Her smile spreads as her hand strokes my biceps. "I can help clear your head, if you want."

"No, really, I'm fine," I insist.

"Hey, man!" Luis shouts, wrapping an arm around my shoulder. "You need to loosen up! This is supposed to be fun!" He laughs, his dark brown eyes crinkling at the corners.

"I just don't want to hurt myself again," I say, trying to push thoughts of Kamilla to the back of my mind for now. "But you're right, let's just enjoy the party."

Luis grins, clapping me on the back before rejoining the throng of dancers. I follow him, forcing myself to focus on the present moment, but my thoughts keep drifting back to Kamilla, like a magnet that I can't resist. The more I try to suppress my feelings, the stronger they become.

Chelsea slides up to me, her tight red dress riding up her hips as she grinds her hip against my leg. I fight the urge to cringe.

"You seem like you could use some company," she purrs.

"I'm good," I say, trying to sound appreciative. "I'm just...having an off night, I guess."

"Let me help you with that." She slips her arm through mine and leads me away from the group. I glance back at Luis, who gives me a thumbs-up and a knowing wink.

As Chelsea pulls me closer, guilt rushes through me. The thought of Kamilla's smile, her soft touches, and our stolen kiss haunts me. I can't get her out of my mind. And the more I try to ignore it, the more it gnaws at my core.

The thick scent of alcohol and perfume overwhelms me, making it difficult to breathe. Chelsea, still oblivious to my turmoil wraps her arm around mine, but I'm suffocating. I attempt to take a step back from her and end up plummeting to the floor. Luis is by my side in seconds.

"Jackson," Luis shouts, leaning in to help me stand. "You don't look so good. Maybe we should head out."

"Are you sure?" I ask, looking around at the cheerleaders surrounding us. Part of me wants to stay and forget about Kamilla who will probably run for the hills when she finds out I'm falling for her, but another part – a stronger part – yearns for the quiet solitude of our apartment.

"Absolutely," Luis confirms, resting a hand on my shoulder. "We'll head back to your place, chill out there. Maybe watch a movie or something."

"Sounds good," I agree, but as I start to disentangle myself from Chelsea, Luis holds up a finger.

"Wait," he says, grinning mischievously. "Let's bring Chelsea and some of her friends along. It'll be more fun that way."

Of course.

"I was sorta just hoping it'd just be the two of us," I admit, my heart sinking. The last thing I want is to prolong this night surrounded by people I don't want to entertain, especially when all I can think about is Kamilla. But how do I explain that to Luis who is jumping through hoops to entertain his best friend he believes has been trapped inside an apartment with a woman who hates his guts.

"Come on, man," Luis urges. "It'll take your mind off things. You need to relax and have some fun."

I sigh, knowing that resisting Luis's insistence would be futile. "Alright, fine. Just a few people though, okay?"

"Deal," Luis agrees before whispering something to Chelsea and two of her friends. "Ready to go?"

"Ready as I'll ever be," I reply, forcing a smile onto my face. But deep down, I know that no amount of distraction can truly erase the image of Kamilla from my thoughts.

Luis wraps his arm around one of the cheerleaders with a grin as we make our way down in the elevator and away from the hotel.

The music from the party still echoes in my ears as we enter my apartment, the group of cheerleaders following closely behind. I glance around the room, filled with people I barely know, and struggle to find the enthusiasm Luis expects me to have.

"Alright, everyone! Let's get this party started!" Luis exclaims, clapping his hands together. He turns to me, grinning. "Hey Jackson, why don't you whip up some of your signature cocktails? We can play some drinking games, huh?"

I force a smile and nod. "Sure, man."

As I head to the kitchen, I do my best to focus on the task at hand, but Kamilla remains a constant on my mind.

"Here, let me help you," Chelsea says, appearing beside me. She leans against the counter, her blonde hair cascading over her shoulders, framing her slender face. Her blue eyes lock onto mine, a sultry smile playing at the corners of her lips. "So, Jackson... What's the deal with you and Luis's little sister? She seems to talk a lot about you in our sessions."

My ears perk up at the mention of Kamilla's name, but the mischievous look on Chealsea's face tells me enough to know that nothing coming from her mouth is true. I'm not exactly sure what angle she's playing at or why that would be any of her business if we were. But I have zero intention of disclosing anything about Kamilla to her.

"Really?" I ask, trying to sound interested as I mix the drinks.

"Uh-huh," she purrs, inching closer. "Kamilla's always talking about what an amazing guy you are. And how hot you are with your shirt off. So, are you guys like sleeping together or whatever?"

"Is that so?" I reply, handing her a drink. The ice clinks against the glass as she takes a sip, never breaking eye contact. It's clear she's trying to seduce me, but I can't tell if it's for information or plain stubbornness. Either way, she's barking up the wrong tree.

"Let's join the others and play those drinking games, shall we?" I suggest, trying to put some distance between us.

"Sounds fun," Chelsea agrees, looping her arm through mine as we make our way back to the living room.

Luis has already set up a game of Kings Cup, and I roll my eyes as he explains the rules with far too much excitement. I play along, adamant to focus on anything than my impulsive thought of coming clean to Kamilla about my feelings. Chelsea tries to slide into my lap and I stand, offering her the seat. It's like I'm in fucking high school all over again, my heart is leading me one way while all rational paired with my guilt for being here with Chelsea, and the mounting pressure from Luis is screaming nothing my heart is telling me is possible.

"Come on, Jackson!" Luis shouts, slapping me on the back. "You're too tense, man! Dance with Chelsea!"

"Uh... sure," I say, without fully hearing his statement. Chelsea grabs my hand, pulling me to the middle of the room. Smiling, Luis switches the TV to music videos. The beat of the music pulses through me, but I'm still disconnected from it all.

"Jackson," Chelsea whispers into my ear, her lips brushing against my skin. "Why don't we go somewhere more private? Like your room?"

Her suggestion sends a shiver down my spine, but not in the way she intends. The thought of being alone with her only makes me feel more guilty, more confused. But what other option do I have? I glance at Luis, who gives me an encouraging nod, and then back to Chelsea's expectant gaze. Being in my room would at least give me some space to sort out my head without Luis's prying gaze.

"Alright," I agree, my voice barely audible. "Let's go."

I lead Chelsea to my room with a heavy heart. It's like I'm walking through quicksand. Each step closer to the door brings more guilt and confusion that I can't shake off.

As we enter the dimly lit bedroom, Chelsea's fingers brush

against mine as she closes the door behind us. She saunters over to the TV and picks up the remote control. I watch her, unsure of what to expect, my hands fidgeting at my sides.

"Let me set the mood," Chelsea purrs, turning on the television. The screen flickers to life, displaying a pornographic scene. The moans and gasps from the TV echo through the room, making it even more uncomfortable.

"Is this really necessary?" I ask, trying to swallow the lump in my throat.

"Trust me, Jackson," she replies, a sultry smile playing on her lips. "It'll help you relax."

But the opposite is true. As the explicit images play out on the screen, my thoughts only grow more tangled. How could I let myself be led into this situation? And why am I still here when all I want is to be with Kamilla?

Chelsea approaches me, running her fingers along my chest. Her touch sends a shiver down my spine, but not in the way she intends.

"You're so tense," she whispers, pressing her body against mine. "Let me help you unwind..."

My mind races, searching for a way out of this predicament. But just as I'm about to voice my reluctance, a thought occurs: *Maybe if I give in to Chelsea's advances, I can finally put an end to my inner turmoil. Perhaps this is what I need to forget about any emotional connection with Kamilla and back to the casual sex she wants.*

"Okay," I say, feigning enthusiasm. "Let's do this."

A bead of sweat trickles down my temple, the tension in the room suffocating. Chelsea's lips press against my forehead, but I feel nothing, only the echo of Kamilla's intoxicating kiss still lingering in my memory.

"Jackson, relax," Chelsea breathes into my ear, as she begins unbuttoning my shirt. I force a smile, trying to shake off my inner conflict. But no matter how hard I attempt to focus on the moment, my thoughts keep drifting back to Kamilla.

"Maybe we should try something different?" I suggest, hoping a change will help me get into it.

Chelsea's face lights up with a smirk.

"Alright then," she says, guiding me to a chair in the corner of the room. "Sit down and let me take care of you."

I obey, settling into the chair as Chelsea straddles my lap, her hips swaying to an imaginary rhythm. She runs her hands through my hair and grinds against me, trying her best to turn me on. But all I can think about is the way Kamilla's eyes sparkled when she laughed, the warmth of her touch, the softness of her skin.

"Jackson, what's wrong? You seem...distracted," Chelsea murmurs, her frustration evident.

"Sorry," I mumble, attempting to hide my true feelings. "Just a lot on my mind, I guess."

"Let me help you forget," she whispers, nibbling on my earlobe. Despite her efforts, my body remains unresponsive, my desire for Kamilla refusing to be extinguished.

"Chelsea, I'm sorry, but this isn't working for me," I finally admit, unable to keep up the charade any longer. "I just can't get into it."

Her face falls, hurt flashing across her eyes before she quickly masks it with a forced smile. "Oh, have you started having issues getting it up. Lots of men struggle with that. I can totally help you with that."

My jaw clenches at her suggestion of impotence. Chelsea, oblivious to my shift in mood, stands and proceeds to do the most awkward dance I've ever seen while struggling to unbuckle the top of her bra type cheer top.

What in the actual fuck?

CHAPTER 18

The jingle of my keys announces my entrance as I step into the living room of our apartment. The sight of Luis lounging on the couch with two cheerleaders from his NFL team draped over him greets me. I roll my eyes, resisting the urge to groan at the cliché scene playing out in front of me.

"Hey, sis," Luis grins, seemingly unfazed by my obvious disapproval. "Sorry, plans changed. Jackson wasn't feeling the party."

My gaze flicks between him and the cheerleaders giggling at every word he says. Their ridiculously short skirts barely cover their thighs. It's not that I'm against women wearing whatever they want, but something about this entire situation just rubs me the wrong way.

'Thrilling," I reply, dropping my bag on the floor and making my way to the kitchen. "There goes my night of peace."

"Aw, don't be like that," Luis calls after me. "We're just celebrating our main man being back on the green."

"By turning our living room into a frat house?" I mutter under my breath, but don't bother arguing further. Instead, I focus on grabbing a glass of water from the tap, trying to tune out the muffled female voice coming from the other room.

I take a sip, the agreement Jackson and I made at the front of my mind. We agreed to casual. So, I have no right to focus on the jealously rising in the pit of my stomach. No right to have believed that the way he made love to me last night meant he was ready for something more than just sex, but I'd been hopeful. Stupid, more like it, especially now that I know he's just beyond that door, undoubtedly occupied with another woman.

I shake my head, trying to clear those thoughts away. This is what Jackson wanted, isn't it? What I wanted? To be sexually satisfied without the hassle of the heart involved. Except for I messed up, because I opened my heart despite knowing I shouldn't have.

"Kamilla, come join us!" one of the cheerleaders calls out, waving a hand in my direction. "We're about to start a round of Never Have I Ever!"

"Sounds like a blast," I lie, forcing a smile as I step back into the living room. It's not an ideal situation, but for now, I'll just have to push through it as the last place I want to be is on the other side of that wall.

Luis grins over at me. "You did a fantastic job with Jackson, you know? He would've never been cleared this quickly without your help. You guys must've really been going at it."

I narrow my eyes at him, trying to decipher what he was getting at. "Yeah, well, 'going at it' as you put it is what I do. I just gave him guidance on how to treat his injuries."

"Guidance, huh?" Luis smirks, winking at me before pointing towards Jackson's closed bedroom door. The unmistakable sound of moans drifts through the air, making my cheeks flush with a mixture of embarrassment and jealousy. "Seems like he's taking your advice to heart. He's finally letting loose and having fun again."

My stomach churns as I clench my fists, doing my best to suppress the surge of envy threatening to consume me. It's ridiculous, really. I shouldn't care about what Jackson does in his private life. We had an agreement, and that was all there was to it.

"Right," I force out, plastering a fake smile on my face. "Good for him." I take a deep breath, trying to focus on the present moment rather than the sounds coming from Jackson's bedroom.

"Damn straight," Luis says, turning his attention back to the cheerleaders who fawn over him. "You're always looking out for people, Kamilla. That's one of your best qualities."

"Thanks, I guess," I respond, hugging myself. For some reason, his words don't hold the same comfort they usually would.

The sound of the chatter and moans from behind Jackson's door make it hard to concentrate on anything else. I think back to the way Jackson made love to me last night. It had felt so real, so passionate.

"Hey, are you okay?" Luis asks, his voice laced with concern.

"Of course," I lie, forcing a tight-lipped smile. "Why wouldn't I be?"

He studies me for a moment before shrugging. "I don't know, you just seem...off."

"Oh. It's just some stuff at the clinic. Nothing I can't handle," I assure him, though the jealousy gnawing at my insides begs to differ. Once again, my mind drifts back to the agreement Jackson and I made. We promised to keep things strictly sexual with no emotions or attachments. And for good reason. We lived different lives. I'm focusing on my career. While Jackson, well, is focused on things outside of relationships.

"Alright, if you say so." Luis seems unconvinced, but he doesn't push further. Instead, he takes a swig from his beer and returns his attention to the cheerleaders.

"Chelsea is really going at it," one of the cheerleaders says, smirking as the moans intensifies. "What do you think is going on in there?"

"I don't know, and frankly I don't care," I say, irritation bleeding into my tone.

"Come on Kam," Luis says, raising an eyebrow. A cheeky grin spreads across his face. "You can't tell me you're not the least bit curious about what's going on in there. I mean, how many girls can say they were the reason for Jackson Taylor's return to his 'prime'?"

My hands clench into fists at my sides. It's clear that he's trying to get under my skin, and it's working. He always gets like this when he's trying to prove a point. But what's his point here, anyway? That Jackson's an ass who flip flops in his emotional connections? Newsflash, I already know that a bit too well.

"Can we please just drop it? I don't want to talk about Jackson, or anything related to what the hell goes on in that room," I snap, my voice tight.

"Alright, alright," he chuckles, holding up his hands in mock surrender. "I'm sorry, okay. I didn't mean to upset you."

"Whatever," I mutter, turning my attention back to the movie playing on the screen. But as much as I try to lose myself in the plot, I remain hyper-aware of every little sound coming from Jackson's bedroom – each moan, each sigh, each gasp tearing through me like a dagger.

"Why did I have to get stuck living with an asshole that doesn't understand boundaries," I mutter, storming out of the living room, leaving Luis and the cheerleaders behind. My heart is pounding in my chest, and tears threaten to spill over as I make my way to my bedroom, slamming the door shut behind me.

"Kamilla, you're better than this," I whisper to myself, fighting back tears. "You don't have to put up with this."

I refuse to shed a tear. I refuse to give Jackson the satisfaction. Releasing a deep breath, I grab a duffle bag and start stuffing clothes in. I can't stay here right now. I don't trust myself to face Jackson after all this. I need time to sort out my emotions.

"Fuck it," I say, reaching for my phone. The moans continue, louder and more desperate, and my own desperation grows alongside them. I need to get out of here. I need to feel safe again.

My fingers tremble as I tap the call button in the Sisterhood chat. As the ringing fills my ears, I pace back and forth.

"Hey girl, what's up?" Natasha's voice is a welcome relief when she finally answers.

"I know you bitches missed me," Trina chipped in, laughing.

"Hey, hey," Latalia jumped on. "Considering this was a voice call, I'm assuming somethings on fire. Is everyone okay?"

A bitter laugh escapes my lips. "I guess we could say my life is on fire." I sigh. "Guys... I need a favor. I can't get into it over the phone, but I can't stay here tonight. Can I stay with one of you for a few days? I'll crash on the couch or something?" My voice cracks.

"Honey, of course," Trina. "Latalia's old room is still just storage, we can empty it and you can stay here for as long as you need. But are you okay? Is it safe to leave where you are? Are you at home?" Trina's concern is palpable, even through the phone.

"I'm fine. It's just... things at the apartment have become unbearable. I can't take it anymore." I choke back a sob, unwilling to delve into the details just yet.

"Say no more," Latalia cuts in. "Get out of there. Let's all meet up at Tri's place. Nat and I will help move the stuff from t0 my old room to the living room and we can make it into a girl's night hang."

"That's what I was thinking too," Natasha adds.

"Thanks, guys. Really. I'll be there as soon as I can."

"Drive safe," Trina says. "I'll set up the mini bar. Talk more when you guys get here."

With that, I hang up the call, a small but significant weight lifting from my shoulders. Focused, I slip my phone into my pocket, throw on my duffle and head out as fast as I can.

The pounding in my chest hasn't eased, and I can barely catch my breath as I buzz up to Trina's apartment. A tight feeling constricts around my throat. I recall Jackson's bedroom door, locked, and the sound of moans filling our shared apartment. I close my eyes for a moment and swallow the pain. I feel lost.

The door swings open when I get to Trina's apartment door and three pairs of concerned eyes greet me. Both Latalia, and Natasha got here before me. Their expressions mirror my insides. Trina holds the door open wider. I walk in with unshed tears burning my eyes and they envelope me in a four-way bear hug. Their comforting embrace is enough to squeeze the first tear from my eyes.

"It's alright, honey," Latalia whispers. "We're here for you."

The four of us sit down on the couch in Trina's living room. The apartment is always warm, homey. I sniffle, looking at my friends, and try to muster a smile. Natasha reaches over and grabs my hand.

"So, what's going on, Kam?" Natasha asks.

The floodgates break as the words pour out of my mouth. I tell them everything: about the friends-with-benefits agreement I had with Jackson, how I'd been feeling lately, and what I'd heard in our apartment. I look down, ashamed. "I'm such an idiot," I mutter under my breath. "I shouldn't have gotten involved in the first place. It was meant to be professional, and now, I've gone and caught feelings."

Latalia shakes her head firmly. "Don't say that. You're human, and humans have feelings. It's normal."

Natasha nods. "Yeah, you can't help who you fall for."

I sigh. "I don't know what to do."

Trina leans forward. "First things first, I know we hate his guts right now, but you need to talk to him, Kam."

My eyes widen. "No way! I can't do that. Did you not hear

what I said? I came home and heard them moaning in our apartment!"

Trina raises an eyebrow. "And you just assumed it was Jackson?"

"Well, it's his bedroom. Plus made it crystal clear."

Natasha chimes in, "Kamila, you should at least give him a chance to explain. Maybe it's not what you think. You also thought he'd been sleeping around and that turned out to be something else."

I shake my head, sighing. "I don't want to get hurt, guys."

Latalia looks at me with compassion in her eyes. "Life is full of risks. Sometimes, you have to take them, even if they might hurt. This could be something real. Don't let your fear of getting hurt stop you from pursuing something that could be beautiful."

I nod slowly, the words sinking in. Maybe they're right. Maybe I should give Jackson a chance to explain. Just not right now.

We sit in silence for a few moments, each lost in thought. The energy in the room feels lighter, like a weight has been lifted.

Latalia looks at me and smiles. "It's okay to fall for someone, Kamila. It's okay to be vulnerable. That's what makes us human. You don't have to talk to him now, but he deserves to at least know how you feel this time around. When you're ready."

I smile back, the tiniest glimmer of hope peaking through in my heart.

Latalia pops open a bottle of red wine and pours me a glass.

Natasha leans forward, her eyes mischievous. "So, how about we talk about something less serious for a change? Like that guy Trina's been telling me about at work, the one who's been flirting, and might ask her out."

I laugh, my spirits lifting as I take a sip.

Trina scoffs, but if I didn't know better, I'd say she legit blushed. "First of all, he's not some guy. He's, my boss. And there's nothing to tell because I don't sleep with people from work. I got rules of my own remember."

The mood in the room shifts, and the conversation turns to lighter topics. As we sit, drink and chat, my thoughts of Jackson drift to the back of my mind. I know I'll eventually have to hear Jackson out. But it sure as hell won't be today and it may not even be tomorrow. When it happens, it'll be on my terms.

CHAPTER 19

JACKSON

Chelsea slams the bedroom door behind her, leaving a trail of expletives in her wake. I can still hear her grumbling under her breath as she storms out of my apartment. Her bitter expression is burned into my memory, but truth be told, I don't care. My heart longs for Kamila, not some shallow fling with my egotistical ex.

"Chelsea stormed out," Luis says, standing as I enter the living room. "What happened?"

"Nothing worth talking about," I mutter, trying to downplay the situation. "I just told her the truth... I'm not interested in her."

Luis sighs. "Damn man, I wish you'd told her that at another time when I didn't have to do the gentleman thing and see them home safe."

I shrug. "I needed her to hear me. I've already tried other ways."

"Ah, I see." Luis nods. "Alright bro. I better get out there. I'm in for an earful on the ride back."

As soon as the door clicks shut, a pang of uncertainty swirls in my chest. I pace the length of the apartment. Kamilla is normally home by this time. Maybe she got a last-minute client. Or maybe she's out on a date. The thought makes my stomach turn.

"Get a grip, Jackson," I mutter under my breath, stopping by the window and peering into the city lights below. My hands rest on the windowsill, knuckles turning white as I grip it tightly, trying to ground myself. I need to find a way to show Kamila that I'm serious about us – that I'm not just another guy looking for a fling. But how?

"Surprise her," I say aloud, an idea starting to take shape. A romantic dinner, something intimate and meaningful. It might be a cliché, but it feels like the right direction. I want to create an atmosphere where she can feel safe and cherished, where we can talk openly and honestly about our feelings.

"Alright," I tell myself. "Let's do this."

I shoot Kamilla a text message.

Me:

We should talk when you get home. It's important.

No response comes right away, but that's normal if she's with a client. I head for the kitchen and begin gathering ingredients, planning a menu that I can manage to make and will impress her. While cooking, I let my thoughts wander, imagining Kamila's reaction to the evening's surprise and my confession.

"Focus on the present," I remind myself, sighing as I move to chop vegetables. Tonight, is about showing her that I'm willing to go the extra mile for a real relationship. That's what matters.

An hour and a half later, the table is set, and the apartment is bathed in the soft glow of candles strategically placed throughout the room. The flickering light dances across the meticulously set table, adorned with a bouquet of roses – Kamila's favorite flowers and their rich, velvety scent fills the air. I step back to admire my handiwork.

"Kamila's going to love this," I whisper to myself, trying to quell the butterflies fluttering in my stomach. Moments later, my phone chimes with a text message. My heart leaps, but it's just Luis checking in to let me know things mellowed down with Chelsea and he got home safe.

Another two hours pass by, and the candles burn lower. The food sits untouched, growing cold on the table. Kamila's absence gnaws at me, her silence twisting like a knife in my gut. My phone feels heavy in my hand as my fingers hover over her number.

"Where are you, Kammie?" I send another text, the previous ones left unanswered. I pace the floor, my thoughts racing with every passing minute.

"Did I come on too strong? Was this too much?" I mutter, raking my fingers through my hair.

"Damn it, Jackson," I scold myself, clenching my fists. "You're supposed to make her feel special, not smothered."

"Hey," I send one more text, the desperation seeping into my words. "I'm worried about you. Please let me know if you're okay."

Time ticks by, and the once inviting atmosphere of the apartment grows oppressive. The candlelight casts eerie shadows across the walls, mocking my efforts to create a romantic evening. I slump onto the couch, my head sinking into my hands.

"Maybe Luis was right," I admit, my chest tightening with the sting of defeat. "Maybe Kamila deserve better than me, and everyone can see it but me."

Sighing, I dial her number again.

"Come on, Kamila," I whisper to myself as I dial her number for what feels like the hundredth time. My heartbeat accelerates with each ring, my chest tightening.

"Hello?" a voice finally answers, but it's not the one I've been longing to hear.

"Natasha?" I ask, my fingers gripping the phone, relief filling me that Kamilla is at least okay.

"Stop calling," she snaps, her tone dripping with disdain. "Kamila can't come to the phone right now."

"Where is she? Is she okay?" My concern overpowers any irritation at Natasha's attitude.

"None of your business," she retorts, and I can practically see her rolling her eyes through the phone. "You really messed up this time, Jackson."

"Look, I know I screwed up not talking to her last night, but I need to talk to her." My voice cracks. "Please, let me explain."

"Explain?" another voice chimes in. Trina? "What's there to explain? You're just another man who thinks he can play with her feelings and get away with it."

"That's not true. I care about her." The words tumble out, raw and desperate. "I just want to make things right."

"Save it, Jackson," yet another voice hisses. This one I know is Kamilla's friend, Latalia. "Kamila deserves better than you."

"Wait—" I begin, but the line goes dead before I can say anything more.

My hand falls to my side, the phone slipping from my grasp and clattering onto the floor. It feels like a punch to the gut, the air stolen from my lungs.

"Damn it," I curse under my breath, my frustration boiling over. I run my hands through my hair, tugging at the roots. How am I supposed to fix this if nobody will give me the chance?

"Kamila," I whisper, my voice barely audible over the pounding of my heart. "Please, just give me a chance to prove that I'm not like the others."

But as I stand there in the dim light of the apartment, my words echoing into the emptiness, it's clear that actions will speak louder than any apology. I need to find a way to show

Kamila how much she means to me, even if it feels like the world is conspiring against us.

"These women don't know everything," I remind myself, determination flooding through my veins. "I won't let them define who I am or what I feel for Kamila."

And with that resolve, I pick up my phone and begin searching for a way to make things right. It won't be easy, but I owe it to Kamila—and myself—to try.

CHAPTER 20

JACKSON

Seven days. It's been seven fucking days since Kamilla's been home. Seven days with her ignoring my calls and screening her clinic visits. My chest clenches as I stand on the edge of the football field, my heart pounding with uncertainty. The hurt and confusion within me feel like a storm brewing in my gut, making it hard to breathe. Kamilla's absence has left a void that seems impossible to fill, and I find myself questioning everything.

I shake my head, trying to focus on the present. This field is familiar territory, and I need to get back to my old routine – football practice, gym sessions, and pushing my body to its limits. I can't let this inner turmoil consume me. I have to ignore my feelings for Kamilla. There's no room for distractions if I want to regain my optimal performance.

"Jackson!" Coach Thompson calls out, snapping me back to reality. "You're up!"

"Right," I mutter under my breath as I jog onto the field. My cleats dig into the turf, and I give myself a mental pep talk. This is what I'm good at; this is where I belong.

"Alright, team! Let's run the play we worked on yesterday," Coach says, his voice booming across the field. The sound of claps and shouts of encouragement from my teammates surround me, but they fade into the background as I take my position.

"Blue 42! Blue 42! Set, hut!" I shout, the ball snapping into my hands. My muscles tense as I scan the field, searching for an open receiver. The pressure mounts, and I remind myself, "This is just practice. You've done this before, Jackson."

"Downfield!" a teammate yells, and I spot him racing forward, arms outstretched. With a deep breath, I hurl the ball with all my might, hoping for the best.

"Nice!" he exclaims, catching the ball with ease and diving into the end zone. The team erupts in cheers, but I'm not satisfied. The throw wasn't perfect. It was forced, lacking the usual fluidity and ease.

"Good job, Jackson," Coach Thompson praises me, clapping me on the back. "Keep working on that arm strength, and you'll be unstoppable."

"Thanks, Coach," I reply, my voice strained. It takes every ounce of willpower not to let my frustration show. This isn't enough; I need to do more.

After practice, I head straight to the team gym, determined to push myself harder. My body aches as I start with bench presses, the weights heavy in my hands. Sweat trickles down my temples, blurring my vision, but I power through the pain. The rhythmic clang of metal against metal fills the air, drowning out my thoughts.

"More weight," I grunt, forcing myself to add another plate. The burn intensifies, consuming me, but my mind stubbornly drifts back to Kamilla. How her hands felt on my skin during our therapy sessions, the warmth of her smile, the way her eyes sparkled when she laughed.

"Damn it," I curse under my breath, slamming the weights back onto the rack. No matter how hard I try to focus on my routine, Kamilla haunts me like a ghost I can't exorcise. I can't keep doing this to myself. I have to find a way to move past these feelings, or they'll consume me entirely.

"Come on, Jackson!" Luis shouts from beside me, spotting my bench press. "You got this!"

But each rep feels like an uphill battle, my body protesting against the strain. Damn it, why can't I shake these thoughts?

"Enough," I gasp out, racking the barbell and sitting up, wiping the sweat from my face. "Let's move on."

"Alright, man," Luis agrees, concern furrowing his brow. "You're pushing yourself pretty hard today."

"Need to get back in shape," I mutter, avoiding his gaze. The truth is, I'm desperate to bury myself in my training, to regain control over my life and forget about the emotional chaos that Kamilla has thrown me into.

As we hit the next set of exercises, my phone buzzes with a message. My heart leaps – maybe it's Kamilla? But no, it's just a text from Chelsea, asking how my day was going. I reply with a short message, not wanting to admit my growing loneliness.

"Chelsea?" Luis asks, noticing the exchange.

"Yeah, just checking in." I force a smile, but it doesn't reach my eyes.

"Hey, let's grab some dinner after this, yeah?" Luis suggests, no doubt in an attempt to lift my spirits. "My treat."

"Sure," I agree, though the thought of food does little to satisfy the hunger gnawing at me.

The gym's fluorescent lights seem harsher and colder as we finish our workout, and I find myself longing for the soothing warmth of Kamilla's hands on my skin. But I shake my head, banishing the memory. I can't afford to dwell on her right now – not when my football career is hanging in the balance.

"Yo, you're zoning out again," Luis chides me gently. "What's going on, man?"

"Nothing," I lie, forcing another smile. "Just tired."

"Alright," he says, unconvinced but letting it go for now. We walk towards the gym exit, and I try to muster some enthusiasm for dinner with my best friend. But deep down, I know that no amount of food or conversation will fill the void inside. And as much as I try to push Kamilla from my mind, I still wonder when she'll be back – and if things between us will ever be the same again.

Dinner and the rest of the day goes by in a blur. I lie on my bed, staring at the ceiling. Darkness envelops the room, and it feels as if it's closing in around me, suffocating me. I can't escape the thoughts that keep racing through my mind – thoughts of Kamilla, and how much I miss her touch, her frustration, her presence. I know I'm supposed to be focusing on my career, and recovery, but all I can think about is her.

"Get a grip, Jackson," I mutter to myself, trying to shake off the overwhelming sense of loneliness that has taken hold of me. I close my eyes, trying to push away the hopelessness that threatens to overwhelm me. What am I supposed to do now? How can I move forward when every step I take seems to lead me back to Kamilla?

"Dammit," I whisper, my voice cracking. I never thought I'd be this guy – the one who's brought to his knees by a woman. But here I am, a complete mess, trying to make sense of emotions that seem beyond my control.

In a last ditch effort of connecting with Kamilla I reach for my phone and shoot her yet another message.

Me:

Can we please just meet somewhere and talk? I'm not sure what I did to scare you off, but I promise you if it hurt you enough for you to leave it'll never be done again. Luis insists that you're just spending a few days with your friend that's going through something. But in my gut, I know there's something wrong as you won't even talk to me, and your friends made it clear I'm not the man for you. But, please, I swear I just want to talk.

SIGHING, I hit send, but after about twenty minutes without a response I stuff the phone beneath my pillow and allow sleep to consume me.

CHAPTER 21

KAMILLA

The sound of the door unlocking echoes through Jackson's apartment, making me freeze for a moment. I take a deep breath and push it open, steeling myself for the memories that assault me as I cross the threshold. The place is quiet. Jackson should be at practice this time of day which makes it the perfect time to slip in and collect my things before leaving his life for good.

"Kammie?"

I jump at the sound of Jackson's voice and turn around to find him standing in the doorway, looking as bewildered as I feel. His dark brown hair is tousled, his muscles evident beneath the plain white T-shirt he's wearing.

'Jackson," I say, trying to keep my voice steady. "I didn't think you'd be here. I just came to get my stuff."

'What's going on, Kammie?" he asks, folding his arms across his chest. "Why have you been avoiding me? It's like a slap in the face and I don't even know what I did to deserve it."

My heart clenches at his words, and I suppress the urge to lash out at him. He's the one who's betrayed me, and yet he wants to discuss my behavior? I shove my hands into the pockets of my jeans, trying not to let my anger show.

"Maybe if you learned to control your dick, you'd know why I'm upset," I retort, my voice strained.

"Ever since we made love, you've been distant and cold," he says, his eyes searching mine. "You're pulling away from me, Kamilla, and I don't understand why."

I scoff, his words mixing disbelief with my anger. How can he stand there and act as if he's the victim when he's the one who's been sleeping around?

"Oh, I know you are not putting this all on me after you broke down my walls and made me feel things for you, even after I tried so desperately not to. Only to then turn around and fuck a cheer-leader the next day," I snap, unable to hold back my emotions any longer.

"Cheerleader?" he asks, his eyebrows furrowing in confusion. "What are you talking about?"

"Don't play dumb with me," I reply, my voice shaking. "You asked me to let go, to trust you, and I did. Then you ignore me to go sleep with them!"

"Kamilla, I don't know what you're on about, but I assure you its not true," he says, taking a step towards me.

I step back.

"I haven't slept with anyone else since you moved in," he says.

I stare at him, trying to read his expression. Part of me wants to believe him, but the hurt and betrayal make it difficult to trust anything he says.

"Kamilla, please trust me when I say that I haven't been with anyone else since you moved in," he pleads, desperation seeping into his voice. "I've been trying so hard to respect your bound-aries and not push you into something you're not ready for."

The weight of Jackson's gaze presses down on me as I struggle to digest his confession. My heart races, torn between longing and fear. The air feels heavy, charged with emotions that threaten to consume us both.

"Jackson..." I whisper, my voice barely audible, as I search for the words to express the turmoil within me. "I want to believe you; I really do but... I've been hurt before. Plus, I know what I heard. And if that wasn't a big enough slap in the face Luis and your little girlfriends painted a really vivid picture for me."

The expression on his face falls and he runs a hand through his dark hair. "I don't know what they told you, but nothing happened between me and Chelsea in that room. I swear on all things I hold dear. Her being in that room with me wasn't even my idea. What they heard out here was a wack ass porno that she switched on before I kicked her ass out. Ask Luis if you need confirmation, but I'm telling you the truth."

Jackson's hand travels to my face as he steps closer. "Chelsea is my past, Kamilla. And hopefully now she gets that through her head. You are who I want in my present and future."

I blow out a shaky breath, fighting the urge to melt into his arms.

"Tell me you feel nothing for me, and I swear I'll walk away," Jackson growls.

I meet his eyes, tears threatening to escape. "I've followed my heart blindly before, and from experience, that doesn't end well. I don't know if I can trust my feelings anymore."

His grip on my face tightens, a flicker of pain flashing across his eyes. "Kamilla, please," he whispers. "Let me show you that what I feel for you is real. That I'm not like those who have hurt you in the past."

I close my eyes, trying to ignore the magnetic pull I feel toward him. As much as I want to lose myself in Jackson's embrace, I can't open my heart up to someone who isn't ready to receive it. And based on what I've seen, and heard, Jackson isn't ready for a real relationship.

"I'm sorry, I need time," I say, opening my eyes and looking into the depths of his. "Time to sort through my own feelings... and to figure out if I can truly trust you."

He hesitates, our faces mere inches apart, before giving me a slow nod and stepping back.

"Okay," he replies, his voice thick with emotion. "Take all the time you need. Just know that I'll be here, waiting for you whenever you're ready to come back." His eyes lock back onto mine. "I'm all in Kamilla, I want to be with you in a real relationship. And I'll wait for as long as you need to believe that. I'm done hiding."

Again, I close my eyes, before giving in to my urges and doing something I'll regret. Jackson's words echo through my brain as I head to my room to grab some clean clothes and my stuff for work. A part of me wants to believe that he wants a real relationship with me. But I just don't know if I can.

By the time I emerge from my bedroom Jackson is gone. Which is for the best, I tell myself, as the tears I've been holding back from the moment he said my name come streaming down my face.

"Damn it!" I mutter under my breath, rushing through the front door and down the hallway towards the elevator. The cold metal of the button feels foreign against my fingertip as I jam it until the ding sounds. I step inside and lean against the wall, taking deep breaths to calm myself down. I step out of the elevator with my phone in hand, messaging the Sisterhood for a sleepover. Tonight, I need all hands on deck.

CHAPTER 22

JACKSON

The pain on Kamilla's face after I told her how I felt tore me up inside. But I meant every word, and I'm done denying my feelings. I need to come all the way clean before I can fight for anything with Kamilla, and tonight is step one of that.

Mellow jazz music fills the dimly lit bar as I take a seat at the counter, my eyes adjusting to the soft golden hue of the hanging lights. The scent of whiskey lingers in the air as I drum my fingers on the wooden surface.

"Jackson, my man!" Luis exclaims, entering the bar with his signature wide grin. His eyes meet mine. "I've been looking forward to this hang all evening."

"Hey, Luis," I reply, attempting to match his enthusiasm.

We got the week off to rest before diving into our regular intensive training ahead of the season. And though this may not be the best time career wise to blow up my team's chemistry, I can't keep the way I feel about Kamilla from Luis anymore.

I take a swig of my drink. The smooth bitterness of the whiskey helps calm my nerves.

"Actually, Luis, there's something I need to talk to you about," I blurt out.

His smile fades. "Sure, man. What's up?" He leans toward me with genuine interest.

I swallow hard, my throat morphing into sandpaper. "It's about Kamila," I confess, my voice a mere whisper.

"Kamila?" He raises an eyebrow. "What about her?"

Taking a deep breath, I plunge into the emotional abyss, my heart racing like never before. "Look Luis, I'm going to just spit it out. I've fallen in love with your sister."

The words hang in the air like a thick fog, and for a moment, time seems to freeze. Luis face changes through a cycle of emotions before his jaw clenches in suppressed fury.

A strained laugh leaves his lips. "I swear the drinks in here got me tripping, I could've sworn you just told me you were fucking my sister."

"I didn't," I clarify. "But we have in fact, slept together."

Before I can react, Luis's left fist comes flying toward me. It connects with my jaw, the force of the blow sending me sprawling onto the floor. My head slams against the edge of a nearby table, a sharp pain shooting through my skull. The room spins, and my vision blurs as I struggle to regain my bearings.

"Fuck!" I groan, clutching my throbbing jaw.

A tide of shock and outrage washes over the faces of the bar patrons. They scramble to whip out their phones, eager to capture the drama unfolding before them.

"Yo, break it up!" a guy with a buzz cut bellows, attempting to push his way between Luis and me. My vision is still hazy from the impact, but I can see the concern on his face as he looks down at me.

"Stay the fuck away from my sister!" Luis yells, beer sloshing from his glass. The venom in his voice takes me aback.

"Everybody just chill," the bartender else chimes in, trying to deescalate the situation. "This ain't worth ruining a friendship over."

My head throbs, and my jaw aches, but I force myself to sit up, cringing at the dull pain radiating through my body. The room spins, and I try to focus on my breathing to keep from getting sick.

"Are you alright, man?" asks the bartender, his eyes wide with concern. He reaches for a towel, likely to help clean up any blood.

"Fine," I grunt through clenched teeth, struggling to suppress the humiliation burning inside me. The last thing I want is pity from any of these people. They don't know the truth—only that I've been accused of betraying my best friend by sleeping with his sister.

"I trusted you, man! How could you do this to me?" Luis shouts, his voice cracking.

"Please, it's not what you think, Luis," I plead, my own voice wavering. "If you'd just let me explain."

"Explain? What's there to explain?" He scoffs, stepping back. "You were supposed to be my friend, Jackson. My best friend."

"I am your friend!" I insist. "That's why I'm telling you the truth. Instead of going behind your back anymore."

"Save your explanation for someone who cares," he spits. "Get the fuck out of here, Jackson," Luis snarls, his fists still balled at his sides. His dark eyes bore into mine, hurt and confusion swimming beneath the surface. Nothing I say to him at this point will resonate. So, as much as it kills me, the best thing to do right now is to walk away and let the cards fall where they may.

'Fine," I repeat, pushing myself to my feet. My legs are unsteady beneath me, but I manage to maintain my balance. "I'll go. But I genuinely have strong feelings for Kamilla. This isn't some fling for me."

With my dignity in tatters and my heart heavy, I stumble toward the exit. The whispers and stares of the patrons weigh on me like a lead blanket, but I refuse to let them see me break. My intention coming here was to come clean, and I achieved that. At this point, Kamilla is all that matters. Hopefully that doesn't mean Luis won't be part of my life anymore. But if that's the case then so be it.

CHAPTER 23

ast night was a welcome change. I was able to unwind with my girls and put all the mess and confusion with Jackson toward the back of my mind. I know my worth. I deserve a man that will sacrifice everything for me and scream it to the world. Not to be in a long-term casual fuck buddy scenario that has to be kept hidden. I want more, and this time I need to prioritize myself.

The warm sunlight cascades through the windows of Trina's kitchen, casting a golden glow over our table. I lift my steaming cup of coffee to my lips, savoring the rich aroma before taking a sip. The bitter taste blends with the sweetness of the caramel drizzle, creating a perfect harmony of flavors in my mouth. Trina, Natasha, and Latalia sit across from me, their laughter filling the air after a lewd jokes Trina made about the stupid things men do sometimes.

"Girl, decent guys are hard to find nowadays," Natasha

exclaims, rolling her eyes. "In all honesty though, Kam, I think you should go for it if Mr. Sports Bod wants to commit."

I sigh. "But how can I believe he's really ready to commit when he's given me no proof he even wants something more?"

"Holy shit! Kam, I think you should see this," Trina cuts in, pushing her phone towards me and scrolling through her Instagram feed. "It's all over the internet."

Confused, I glance at the screen. My heart drops. There's a trending video of Luis punching Jackson in a shady ass bar. The caption reads, "Star Quarterback Jackson Taylor got what he deserved."

My breath catches in my throat, and a cold wave of dread washes over me as the scene of Jackson confessing to Luis plays out.

This is about me? What in the actual fuck?

"You okay?" Latalia asks, her voice filled with concern as she notices my reaction to the video.

"Y-yeah," I stammer, struggling to regain my composure. "I just... I don't understand why Luis would do something like that."

"Maybe there's more to the story than meets the eye," Trina suggests, trying to offer some comfort. But my mind races, grasping for answers that refuse to reveal themselves.

"Whatever the reason, I need to talk to both of them," I say. "I can't let this shit show spiral out any further."

"What do you need us to do to help?" Natasha asks, jumping into action. "You know we got your back."

I nod, my hands shaking as I pull out my phone. First, I dial Luis's number, my heart pounding in my chest. It rings several times, but to my dismay, it goes to voicemail. I grit my teeth, trying to quell my frustration.

"Hey, Luis, it's Kamilla. I saw the video of you and Jackson. Like what the fuck was that? Call me back as soon as you can. We need to talk," I say into the voicemail, my voice trembling.

"No answer?" Latalia asks, her brow furrowed.

"Voicemail," I reply.

"Try Jackson," Trina suggests, her dark eyes filled with empathy.

"Right." My fingers move quickly over the screen, dialing Jackson's number. As it rings, I hold my breath, praying that he'll pick up, that he'll be okay. But once again, I'm met with the cold, impersonal greeting of a voicemail inbox.

"Jackson, it's Kamilla. Please call me back as soon as you get this. I'm really worried about you," I say, my voice wavering more than I'd like. I end the call, my heart sinking further.

"Neither of them answered," I tell my friends, my voice a mere whisper.

"Maybe they're busy talking it out?" Trina offers, trying to find a silver lining. But the worry in her eyes tells me she doesn't fully believe her own words.

I sigh. "With my brother's temper, and delusional hold over my life? I doubt that."

"Dammit, Luis!" I mutter under my breath, opening my message app.

Me:
Stay the hell out of my life!
Why would you do something like this?

MY STEPS ECHO off the hardwood floor as I pace back and forth. The silence is suffocating, and my thoughts race with each passing second. I clench my fists, feeling the cold metal of my rings press into my flesh.

"Kam, maybe you should sit down," Trina whispers as I attempt to take deep breaths. My chest tightens.

"Damn you, Luis," I hiss, my voice cracking. "You had no right to interfere." I glance at my phone, willing it to ring or vibrate with some form of response. But it remains silent.

"Ugh!" I groan, my anxiety mounting with each unanswered question. I can't stand this helplessness, this overwhelming need to do something but having no idea where to start. I bite my lip, struggling to keep my emotions in check.

"Kam, it's going to be okay," Trina says, wrapping her arm around me.

"Still nothing?" Latalia asks.

"Nothing yet," I reply, my voice strained as I try to hold back tears.

"Well, whatever's going on, we'll help you through it," Natasha promises, her gaze steady.

"Thank you," I say, my voice thick with emotion. I can't sit still any longer. "I need to go home," I announce, pushing my chair back with a sudden urgency. "Jackson might be there, and I need to make sure he's okay." The words tumble out of my mouth in a rush.

"Alright, let us know if you need anything," Trina says, her voice gentle but firm.

"I will," I reply. My friends nod, and I rush out of the apartment.

My fingers fly over the screen as I compose multiple text messages to Jackson.

Me:
Are you okay?

Me:
Where are you?

· · ·

Me:
Please, Jackson, let me know you're alright.

MY HANDS TREMBLE as I put my phone away and head toward my car. I unlock it and slide into the driver's seat, the familiar smell of lavender surrounding me from my car air freshener.

"Get it together, Kamilla," I mutter under my breath, my fingers gripping the steering wheel. I take a deep breath, willing myself to focus on the task at hand: getting home to Jackson.

The drive is a blur of traffic lights and passing cars, my mind unable to fully process the world around me. All I can think about is getting to Jackson, ensuring his safety, and confronting Luis about his actions.

"Please be there, Jackson," I whisper, my grip tightening on the steering wheel as I approach our building. The sight of it looms before me. I park in the parking lot, my heart pounding like a drum in my chest.

"Here goes nothing," I say to myself, pushing open the car door and stepping out into the evening air. My phone remains silent, but I hold onto the hope that Jackson is inside, waiting for me.

As I approach the apartment door, I notice that it's slightly ajar. A shiver runs down my spine.

"Jackson?" I call out.

No response.

"Jackson, are you here? Please, say something!" I plead, pushing the door open with a trembling hand and stepping inside.

"Kamilla?" Jackson's voice calls out from the living room,

relief clear in his tone. A sob escapes my lips as I rush towards the sound of his voice.

"Jackson. Oh my God. Are you okay?" I ask, my eyes scanning his figure for any bruises or injuries from the fight.

"Other than a bruised ego and a swollen lip, I'm fine," he reassures me, wincing slightly as he touches his mouth. "Luis packs quite a punch."

"God, I was so worried about you," I confess, wrapping my arms around him. "I saw the video and... I thought the worst."

"Hey, it's okay," he whispers, stroking my hair gently. "I'm here, and I'm safe."

"Promise me you won't get involved in something like this again," I demand, looking up into his eyes. "I can't bear the thought of losing you."

"I promise," he replies, pressing a gentle kiss to my forehead. "I don't want to put you through that again."

A smile crosses my lips. "So, based on what you said in the video, you sorta like me, huh?"

Jackson's gaze locked dead onto mine. "I've fallen for you, Kammie. And I'd take a million black eyes before I ever deny it again."

I lowered my lips onto his forehead. "I fell for you too, Jackson."

"God, I wish I could kiss you right now," he growled.

Smiling, I bent over further to plant a light kiss on the side of his lips that isn't swollen.

"As soon as this swelling goes down, I'm claiming those delicious lips of yours. And tonight, if you'll allow me, I love to treat you to an official date."

"You better," I say, a full smile tugging at my lips. "Now let's get you cleaned up Wannabe Muhammed Ali. You'll need some ice on that lip."

"Yes ma'am," he agrees, allowing me to lead him to the bathroom.

EPILOGUE

JACKSON

A year has flown by since our first official date, and Kamilla and I are still inseparable. Our love has grown stronger with each passing day, but today is different. Today, my heart races and my palms sweat as I nervously pace the room, rehearsing the words I want to say to her.

"You've got this," I mumble to myself, trying to steady my racing thoughts and shaky hands. The proposal plan has been eating at me for weeks, and now that the moment is almost here, fear threatens to swallow me whole.

I glance at the small velvet box sitting on the table. It's crazy to think how much my life has changed since having Kamilla move in, and now I can't imagine life without her by my side.

"Hey man, you ready?" Luis's voice startles me out of my thoughts. It took a few months for him to come around. And he actually moved to Phoenix without saying goodbye to me. But once I proved to him that I was serious about being with Kamilla he adjusted to the idea of us being together. He's actually been my rock through all of this, helping me arrange every detail of the perfect proposal. His support means the world to me, especially considering his sister is the best thing that has happened to my life.

"Ready as I'll ever be," I respond, trying to put on a brave face.

"Look, I don't know why," Luis pauses, his laughter filling the room. "But Kam loves you, and you love her. Just let your heart do the talking." Luis gives me an encouraging pat on the back.

"Thanks, man. I really appreciate everything you've done to help," I reply, taking a deep breath.

"Don't mention it, bro," Luis says, leaning against the chest of drawers. "You make my sister happy. I was wrong to have laid hands on you before. At the time, I was up in my feelings and thought I was looking out for a Kamilla's best interest."

"Water under the bridge, man," I'm just happy to still have my best friend and perfect woman in the same lifetime."

"Alright, alright, enough with the sappy shit. I'm gonna go call Natasha to ensure everything is on track to get Kamilla to the football field. Meet you outside in five?"

"Sounds good man," I say, my voice stronger and more resolute than before. It's time to take the leap and ask the woman I love to be my partner for life. And I'm finally ready.

The football field is transformed into a breathtaking wonderland. Twinkling fairy lights drape from goalpost to goalpost, casting a soft glow on the delicate rose petals scattered across the artificial turf. A trail of petals leads to a small stage at the center of the field, adorned with an elegant white archway entwined with lush greenery and vibrant floral arrangements. The air is filled with the sweet fragrance of roses, while a string quartet plays a romantic melody in the background, setting the perfect atmosphere for our big night.

"Wow, Jackson... This is incredible," Luis remarks, looking around in awe as we stand at the edge of the field. "Kamilla is going to love this."

"Thanks, man," I say, a surge of pride rising alongside my nerves. "I couldn't have done it without you."

"Hey, that's what friends are for," he replies, grinning.

"Alright, so let's go over the plan one more time," I suggest, needing the reassurance of having everything in order. "How are we getting Kamilla here without raising suspicion?"

"Already handled," Luis says. "Her Sisterhood told her there's a surprise party for one of our teammates and that she needs to meet us here to help set up. She doesn't suspect a thing."

"Perfect," I say, the knot in my stomach loosening ever a tad. "And she'll be here for seven-thirty, right?" I glance at my watch, it's now seven-fifteen.

"Seven-thirty on the dot," he confirms, holding up his hands in a gesture of surrender. "I promise, Jackson, I've got this under control."

"Okay," I exhale, trying to quell the butterflies fluttering around in my chest. "I trust you. Thank you so much again for doing this."

"Stop thanking me," Luis says laughing. "You're family, and I know how much Kamilla means to you. Now, get out of here and get ready for the big moment. We'll see you back here in a few minutes."

With a final nod, I leave the field, my mind racing as I take my position in the locker room. Not long after Luis call out my signal from the entrance of the field. I glance over, and there she is – beautiful, radiant, and utterly clueless about what's about to happen. Kamilla takes in the sight before her, her expressive eyes widening in surprise, and her hand flies to her mouth, covering a gasp. She looks around, trying to make sense of the magical display as I walk out unto the green.

"Jackson, what is all this?" she asks, stepping closer to me as I come into view.

"Kamilla," I begin, taking a deep breath to calm my nerves. "From the moment I met you, I knew you were special. You're strong, independent, and incredibly passionate about everything you do. Your determination to succeed and your unwavering loyalty to those you love, even when they get on your nerves, are just a few of the many qualities that made me fall in love with you."

I take a step closer, looking deep into her eyes as I continue. "You've changed my life in so many ways. You've shown me the true meaning of love and partnership, and every day with you feels like a gift. I want to spend the rest of my life cherishing you, supporting you, and growing with you. So," I pause to take her hand in mine as her eyes fill with unshed tears. I drop to one knee before her.

I reach into my pocket and pull out the small velvet box. Opening it, I reveal a stunning diamond ring, the band delicately crafted with intricate patterns that seem to dance in the light. The centerpiece is a breathtaking oval-cut diamond, surrounded by a halo of smaller diamonds, creating an ethereal sparkle.

Kamilla gasps, her eyes widening as she takes in the beauty of the ring before her. Her hand flies to her mouth, and for a moment, she is speechless, her gaze locked onto the diamond.

"Kamilla Gabrella Morallez, I love you more than anything in this world, and I want to spend the rest of my life making you happy. Will you marry me?"

"Jackson... I...," she stutters, tears streaming down her cheeks. She takes a deep breath, steadying herself before continuing. "Yes, yes, a million times yes!"

A SURGE of relief washes over me as I slide the ring onto her trembling finger. It fits perfectly. Kamilla throws her arms around my neck as I stand, and I pull her into me for a light kiss.

"I love you so much," she whispers.

"I love you too, baby. We're going to have an amazing life together."

Our friends and family erupt in applause, their cheers filling the night air as we share a tender kiss under the starry sky.

"Forever, Kamilla," I promise her softly, my soul filled with joy as she nods in agreement.

"Forever."

A LETTER TO THE READER

<u>Dear Amazing Human</u>,

Thank you so much for dedicating time out of your life to reading my book! I hope you found it entertaining and were able to have the good time that I had intended it to be.

If you enjoyed what you read, and have a few extra minutes, PLEASE drop a review on Goodreads, Bookbub, and any book retailer of your choice. If you hated it … that sucks. I'd still love to know how I could make your experience better next time. So, please feel free to share your honest thoughts. I'm extremely grateful for you, and I hope you'll join me on the journey of my next release.

By the way, if you'd like to continue along with Jackson and Kamilla to see what they got up to after the story, consider Joining My Newsletter for a bonus epilogue, other free goodies, upcoming release dates and other special offers. *'Bending Her Rules'*, Book 3 in the Rules of Love series is set to release on Novemebr 14, 2023 and is currently available to preorder on all major platforms. So be sure to grab yourself a copy so you can get access to it as soon as it goes live.

Hugs,
    Deidre – Ann Anderson

ACKNOWLEDGMENTS

I want to thank God for blessing me with a fantastic support system and the strength to push forward in spite of it all.

I'm super grateful to my loving husband for all his support, feedback, and encouragement along my journey of losing myself in this story as it consumed me, and rediscovering who I wanted to be. It is impossible to produce a novel without the passion needed not only to write but also to market it. I will be eternally grateful for the pushing force you have been beside me on each leg along the way. I love you, baby!

To all my remaining family members, friends, and readers from across the globe who continue to support me day in and day out, thank you for embracing the magic that evolves out of the craziness in my mind. I am beyond thrilled that you have decided to jump on this winding journey right along with me. Now hang on, as it's about to be a bumpy ride.

ABOUT THE AUTHOR

Deidre - Ann Anderson is a USA Today Bestselling author of everything romance with black women and the men who love them.

She is a Jamaican-born Canadian author who firmly believes that with hard work and dedication, anyone can make a living from what they enjoy.

Deidre – Ann has been a storyteller for most of her life and cannot wait to share all the rigorous love stories of the characters living in her head.

ALSO BY DEIDRE – ANN ANDERSON

CONSUMED BY HEAT TRILOGY

Sparked

Ignited

Engulfed

Falling For Heat - (Clean Version of The Trilogy as A Standalone)

NIGHT CAP NOVELLAS:

Willed to a Dom

The Dom She Needed

RULES OF LOVE SERIES

Changing Her Rules

Breaking Her Rules

Bending Her Rules

THANK YOU FOR ALL YOUR SUPPORT!

To find out more about books, news, and more, sign up to *Dee's Writing Corner*!

*** * * Follow me on the socials * * ***
BookBub
https://www.bookbub.com/authors/deidre-ann-anderson
FB Reader Fam
https://www.facebook.com/groups/
deidreannandersonsreaderfam
TikTok
https://www.tiktok.com/@deidrewritesromance
Author Newsletter
https://view.flodesk.com/pages/64a492bb349daf2cf867bb19
My Author Website
https://www.deidreannanderson.com
Kofi
https://ko-fi.com/autherdeidreannanderson
Instagram
https://www.instagram.com/deidrewritesromance
Facebook

https://www.facebook.com/AuthorDeidreAnnAnderson
Twitter
https://twitter.com/AuthorDeidreAnn
YouTube
https://www.youtube.com/channel/UCI74BpcT-jue7T-SUpwC5rg